"I look upon death to be
as necessary to our constitution as sleep.
We shall rise refreshed in the morning."

—Benjamin Franklin
August 21, 1784

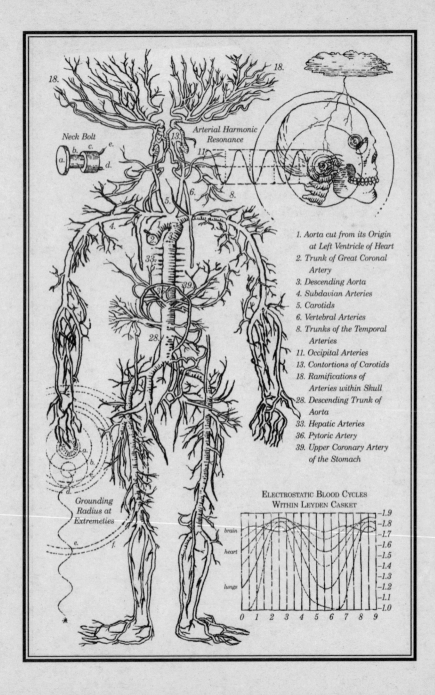

Neck Bolt

Arterial Harmonic Resonance

1. Aorta cut from its Origin at Left Ventricle of Heart
2. Trunk of Great Coronal Artery
3. Descending Aorta
4. Subdavian Arteries
5. Carotids
6. Vertebral Arteries
8. Trunks of the Temporal Arteries
11. Occipital Arteries
13. Contortions of Carotids
18. Ramifications of Arteries within Skull
28. Descending Trunk of Aorta
33. Hepatic Arteries
36. Pytoric Artery
39. Upper Coronary Artery of the Stomach

Grounding Radius at Extremeties

ELECTROSTATIC BLOOD CYCLES
WITHIN LEYDEN CASKET

brain
heart
lungs

0 1 2 3 4 5 6 7 8 9

-1.9
-1.8
-1.7
-1.6
-1.5
-1.4
-1.3
-1.2
-1.1
-1.0

BENJAMIN FRANKLINSTEIN LIVES!

Wherein is contained
an Accounting of the Preparation,
Suspension, and eventual Reawakening of the Subject in Modern Day,
and his Quest to discover the Great Emergency.

BY MATTHEW McELLIGOTT
& LARRY TUXBURY. PHILOM.

Illustrated by Matthew McElligott

SCHOLASTIC INC.
New York Toronto London Auckland
Sydney Mexico City New Delhi Hong Kong

ISBN 978-0-545-35070-9

Copyright © 2010 by Matthew McElligott and Larry Tuxbury.

Illustrations copyright © 2010 by Matthew McElligott. All rights reserved.

Published by Scholastic Inc., 557 Broadway, New York, NY 10012, by arrangement with G. P. Putnam's Sons, a division of Penguin Young Readers Group, a member of Penguin Group (USA) Inc.

SCHOLASTIC and associated logos are trademarks and/or registered trademarks of Scholastic Inc.

12 11 10 9 8 7 6 5 4 3   11 12 13 14 15 16/0

Printed in the U.S.A.   40

First Scholastic printing, February 2011

Design by Matthew McElligott and Katrina Damkoehler

Text set in ITC Cheltenham

The art was done in a combination of traditional and digital techniques.

For Christy, Anthony, and especially to Larry,
a true friend, a fine writer,
and a great American patriot. —M.M.

For Melanie, Nina, and Ella . . .
basically, anyone but Matt. —L.T.

ACKNOWLEDGMENTS
Special thanks to our research consultants:
Dr. Alan Fiero, Rich Lasselle, Dr. Ann "Turtle" Lawrence,
and Larry Tuxbury the Elder.

PROLOGUE
Philadelphia, 1790

KRAK-A-KA-BOOM!

A clap of thunder echoed through the dark, damp basement.

Along the floor, a series of glass jars lined the walls. They glowed eerily, casting their light on the strange, casket-shaped box in the center of the room.

The box rested on a stone pedestal, its thick glass sides framed by gleaming steel. It had been built to last a very long time. A glowing blue liquid pulsated within, like a beating heart.

The old man dipped his hand inside, shivered, and quickly yanked it out. He marveled at the bright fluid dripping from his fingers. Beneath his skin, his veins began to glow—bright, then dim, bright, then dim again.

"The time has come, my faithful friend," he said, smiling grimly at the Custodian. "I am an old man, at death's door. I have little to lose. But you are young. The power that we are about to harness is the power of the heavens themselves. If our calculations are off by only the slightest degree, the results will be catastrophic for both of us. Are you certain?"

The Custodian nodded.

The old man stepped into the open casket and lowered himself halfway into the liquid, which now glowed even brighter. A charge surged deep within his body. It felt as if he were made of electricity itself. He shuddered, spilling liquid over the edge onto the cold floor below.

The Custodian mopped up the mess and wrung it out into a pail. He leaned the mop against the stone wall.

KRAK-A-BOOM!

"I sleep now under your capable care. God willing, I shall *continue* to sleep under the care of your descendants, until the day comes that one of them must awaken me. Their sacrifices will afford me the chance to serve mankind once more, as a citizen of the future."

Two heavy wires hung over the casket from a large metal orb in the ceiling. The Custodian clipped them to bolts that had been surgically implanted into each side of the old man's neck.

KRAK-A-BOOM!

The orb hummed and a jolt of power shot through the old man's veins. He winced and adjusted his high silk collar. The skin on his neck was still sore from the operation, but without the bolts, he would die.

He turned to the Custodian. "My friend, are you absolutely certain? You risk your life."

The Custodian looked into the old man's eyes. "Sir," he said, "you, of all people, should know. Science is risk. Without risk, there can be no progress."

The old man smiled. "Wise words, old friend. *Long live the Modern Order of Prometheus!*"

He fit a copper mask over his nose and mouth and, with a salute, sank into the blue solution.

The Custodian dragged the heavy lid closed, sealing him inside. He walked to the far end of the room, gripped a large metal switch, and waited.

And waited.

And waited.

KRAK-KOW-A-TA-TOW!

Thunder crashed and the Custodian threw the switch. A flash of electricity flooded the room. A loud hum roared through the cables as the liquid glowed fierce and bright. The Custodian shielded his eyes. Sparks exploded from the casket. Test tubes and beakers shattered on the shelves.

And then—it was done.

The Custodian stepped forward cautiously. He studied the body floating in the casket. Was he dead?

No. His chest moved, ever so slightly. He was breathing. Just enough.

It was time to let the old man sleep.

CONSTRUCTION OF THE HARMONIC LEYDEN JAR

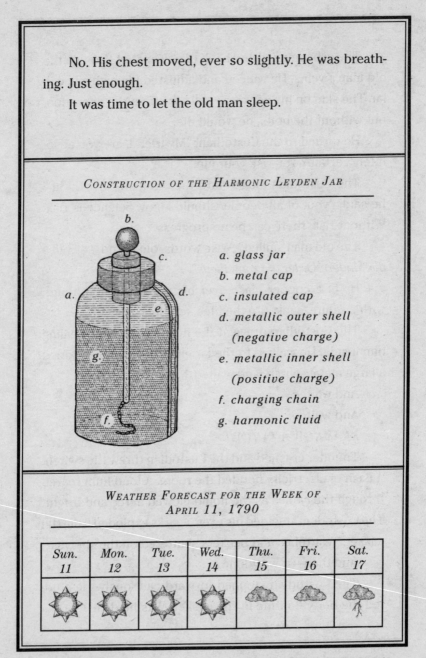

a. glass jar

b. metal cap

c. insulated cap

d. metallic outer shell
(negative charge)

e. metallic inner shell
(positive charge)

f. charging chain

g. harmonic fluid

WEATHER FORECAST FOR THE WEEK OF
APRIL 11, 1790

Sun. 11	Mon. 12	Tue. 13	Wed. 14	Thu. 15	Fri. 16	Sat. 17
☀	☀	☀	☀	☁	☁	🌧

Benjamin Franklinstein Lives!

CHAPTER ONE

Philadelphia, Today

Victor Godwin knew it was going to rain. It didn't matter what the weatherman said. The weatherman was a doofus.

Victor had done the math. He had cross-indexed satellite imagery with data from the National Weather Service. By his calculations, there was a 92 percent chance of a thunderstorm within the next twelve hours.

On TV, the weatherman, Skip Weaver, called for sunny skies as he danced back and forth in front of the weather map. Skip Weaver unbuttoned his shirt. He had painted a big yellow sun with a happy face on his belly and was making it talk by breathing in and out. The other newscasters cheered him on. It was a circus.

This man called himself a meteorologist? A scientist?

Victor dropped his umbrella into his backpack. As usual, he would be the only one at school who had thought to pack one. When would people learn? It was easy to figure out what was going to happen with the weather—or anything, really—if you just paid attention.

He arrived at the bus stop ten minutes before the school bus was scheduled to arrive. Victor had noted that the driver tended to show up anywhere from six minutes early to six minutes late. This gave Victor a buffer of four minutes, which was an acceptable margin of error.

Fifteen minutes later, Scott Weaver arrived. Scott missed the bus at least once a week. This never seemed to bother Scott, but it drove Victor nuts.

"Hey, Victor," said Scott. His shirt was inside out. "Did you catch my dad this morning? Pretty funny, huh?"

Victor glanced up at the sky. It was still clear, but clouds would form soon. "If he were smart," Victor said, "your dad would have painted a big lightning bolt on his stomach instead of a sun."

Scott grinned. "Yeah, that would have been way cool. And he could have painted the rest of his skin red, like the Flash."

Victor shook his head. "That's not what I meant. If he had just checked—"

"Want to see my science project?" Scott interrupted. "It's a potato battery. But I modified it."

"Modified it?"

"Yeah, with paint and stuff, to make it extra powerful. Check it out."

Scott reached down into his backpack and pulled out a shiny object the size of a softball. He tossed it to Victor.

Victor inspected the potato. Some of the paint came off on his hands. "*This* is a potato battery?"

"Well, it's a potato with batteries inside. Like I said, I modified it."

Victor examined the object. It was a huge potato, covered in a thick coat of silver paint. At one end, Scott had scooped out a hole and pressed in a handful of 9-volt batteries. Some of them were leaking a strange gray foam. Victor held it close and sniffed.

"What's that smell?"

"Beats me. I think there's something wrong with the potato. Or it might be the paint. I found it out in the shed. But it looks cool, huh? Like an asteroid."

Victor sighed. "You should always check for chemical interactions before applying an unidentified paint. That way, you'll know exactly what will happen."

"Yeah, I guess you're right." Scott took the potato back from Victor. "It feels kind of hot. Think it's going to explode?"

"Don't be ridiculous," said Victor.

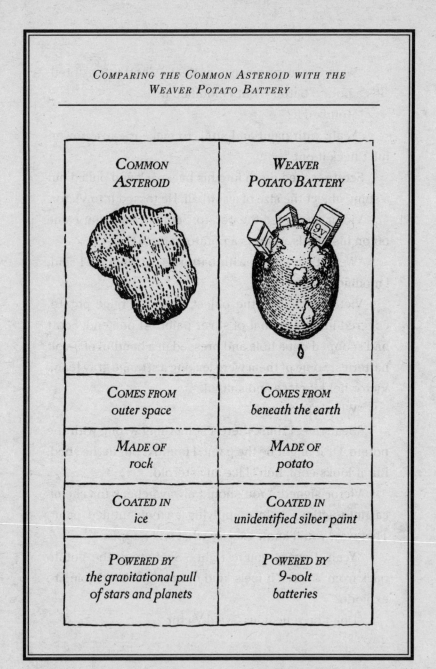

COMPARING THE COMMON ASTEROID WITH THE
WEAVER POTATO BATTERY

COMMON ASTEROID	WEAVER POTATO BATTERY
COMES FROM outer space	COMES FROM beneath the earth
MADE OF rock	MADE OF potato
COATED IN ice	COATED IN unidentified silver paint
POWERED BY the gravitational pull of stars and planets	POWERED BY 9-volt batteries

Benjamin Franklinstein Lives!

CHAPTER TWO
Lightning Strikes

Scott Weaver's potato exploded in the middle of science class.

Technically, it was more of a loud pop, followed by a small, intense fire. It burned a hole straight through the top of his desk. Angela Willbrant said it was the coolest thing she had ever seen.

After school, all the kids wanted Scott to make them an exploding potato. No one wanted to talk about Victor's project: a detailed demonstration of the variable resistance of ceramic insulators. Victor shook it off. It didn't matter what the other kids thought. What mattered was the grade, and his grade was an A. Victor always got an A, except one time in fourth grade when he got an A–. He had vowed never to let that happen again.

By the time he got off the bus home, he was feeling better. He checked the mail and waved to his neighbor Mrs. Vamos, who was out in front of her building, watering her garden. She was always watering her garden, even though it was full of plastic flowers. Several of them still had the price tags attached.

It was ridiculous. Besides, didn't she realize it was going to rain?

Victor set his backpack down on the porch and got out his keys. The FOR RENT sign had blown down again. He propped it back up against the window and let himself in the front door.

Victor paused outside the downstairs apartment. He still half expected Mr. Mercer to pop his head out the door with another corny joke. No matter how bad a day Victor had been having, he could count on Mr. Mercer to cheer him up.

But not anymore. Ever since he passed away last winter, Mr. Mercer's apartment had remained empty. It was a tough place to rent. Theirs was the oldest building on the block, and in the worst condition. Until Victor's mom could afford to fix it up, it was going to stay that way. But until someone moved in, she couldn't afford to fix it up. It didn't seem fair.

There was a note on the kitchen counter:

Working late. Tuna casserole in the fridge.
Don't eat too many cookies.
Love, Mom

Victor felt bad for his mother. It was the third time this week she had to work late.

He ate dinner in front of the TV, then spent the evening in his room working on his volcano. The science fair was coming up in a couple of weeks. He wanted to make sure everything was running perfectly.

Victor had spent the winter studying winning science fair projects from the past twenty years. According to his calculations, a simple baking soda model of Mount Vesuvius, painted brown and covered with miniature scale-model people running for their lives, had a 90 percent chance of winning first prize. If he added at least one graph, he increased the odds by 4 percent. And if the people were wearing togas, and one of them was carrying a dog, it raised them 3 percent more. The judges, typically two-thirds women, apparently loved tragedy. It was a sure thing.

He adjusted a tiny fleeing Pompeiian victim. Outside, the sun was starting to set. Something bothered him. Where were the clouds? If it was going to rain—

KA-BOOOOOOOOM!!!

There was a blinding flash, and the entire house trembled. Victor stumbled back, every hair on his body

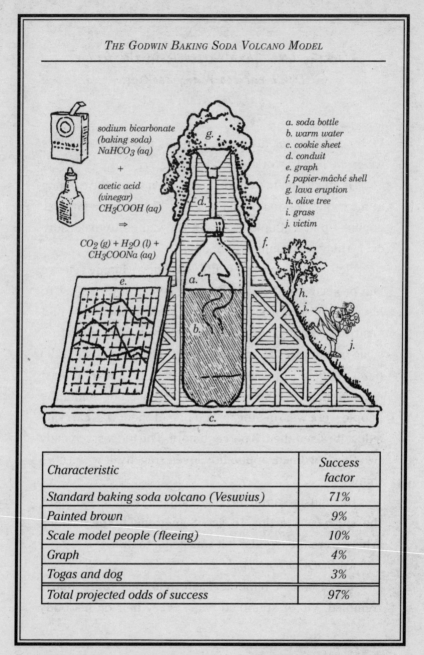

sodium bicarbonate
(baking soda)
$NaHCO_3$ (aq)
+
acetic acid
(vinegar)
CH_3COOH (aq)
$\Rightarrow$

CO_2 (g) + H_2O (l) +
CH_3COONa (aq)

a. soda bottle
b. warm water
c. cookie sheet
d. conduit
e. graph
f. papier-mâché shell
g. lava eruption
h. olive tree
i. grass
j. victim

Characteristic	Success factor
Standard baking soda volcano (Vesuvius)	71%
Painted brown	9%
Scale model people (fleeing)	10%
Graph	4%
Togas and dog	3%
Total projected odds of success	97%

Benjamin Franklinstein Lives!

standing on end. His ears rang. The lights dimmed, and then flickered back to life.

What the heck had just happened? Had lightning hit the house?

He looked out the window. Strangely, the sky was clear. Mrs. Vamos was still watering her plastic garden. Behind her, a man biked down the street. Aside from Victor's frenzied heartbeat, everything seemed normal.

Just the same, Victor went outside to investigate. He knew that in rare cases lightning strikes were possible, even when the sky was clear.

Circling the brownstone, he looked for signs of damage. The paint was peeling. There were cracks in the bricks. The chimney tipped slightly to one side. But none of this was because of the lightning. The building was just old.

As he turned to go back, he spotted something strange. Beneath a coat of flaking red paint, a rusty metal rod ran up the length of the chimney and disappeared over the roof. Funny that he'd never noticed it before. He touched it, and then snapped his hand back. It was hot! The bricks behind it had been scorched black. Was this a lightning rod? If it was, it was unlike any Victor had ever seen.

It was getting dark. He would have to study this more in the morning.

★　★　★

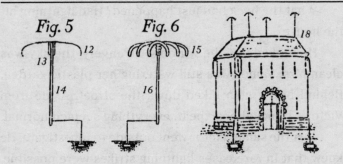

That night in bed, Victor thought about the strange metal rod. There had been dozens of thunderstorms since they had moved in, but lightning had never struck the house before. Why now?

Outside, it was starting to rain, although several hours too late. Victor winced. Scott Weaver's dad *had* painted the right picture on his belly after all.

Victor walked over and shut the window. As he did, he thought he saw something moving out by the sidewalk. A dark, bearlike silhouette, stumbling between the trees. Were those blue sparks crackling around its head?

Victor opened a drawer and rummaged around for a flashlight. He shined it out the window.

Nothing.

Whenever he was tired and alone in the house, his imagination ran wild. A sparking bear?

Ridiculous. It was time for bed.

CHAPTER THREE
A New Tenant

Victor tossed and turned all night. He dreamed of electric bear monsters and lightning storms. By the time he woke up, it was already late morning.

Good thing it wasn't a school day. Still, Victor hated falling behind schedule. He slid open his closet door and unhooked his Saturday hanger, which held the exact same set of clothes the rest of his hangers did: underpants, blue jeans, a gray T-shirt, and white gym socks. A few kids at school made rude comments about him wearing the same thing every day. But not having to decide what to wear saved important brainpower. Brainpower that Victor could use for his scientific pursuits.

After he got dressed and brushed his teeth (up and

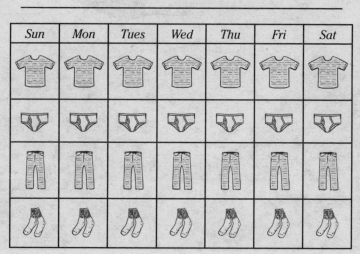

Sun	Mon	Tues	Wed	Thu	Fri	Sat

down thirty-one times), Victor examined his volcano with a magnifying glass. Several blades of grass had tipped slightly during the night, so he straightened them with tweezers. Some people might say it was ridiculous to spend months perfecting a baking soda volcano, but it was this constant attention to detail that would win him first prize.

He could hear people talking downstairs and decided to investigate.

". . . a delightful apartment, Mrs. Godwin. I do believe it will suit me perfectly."

On the landing, Victor's mom was shaking hands with a peculiar old man. He had to be at least eighty, and looked exactly like Benjamin Franklin. He was bald on top, with unruly white hair sticking out from the sides and back of his head. He wore old-fashioned bifocals, a ruffled white shirt and high collar, a red button-down vest, brown pants that were much too short, and white silk stockings that almost met his knees.

"Mom, what's going on?"

Mrs. Godwin turned to her son, beaming. "Victor, I'd like you to meet our new tenant, Mr. Benjamin."

The old man offered his hand to Victor. "Please, call me Frank. How do you do, young man?"

Victor frowned. "Mom, may I speak to you in the kitchen?"

"Victor, shake the man's hand."

Reluctantly, Victor reached out to shake Mr. Benjamin's hand.

"Ouch!" He felt a jolt of electricity and snapped his hand back.

"Oh, dear," Mr. Benjamin said, tugging nervously at his high silk collar. "I do apologize, my boy. The static electricity is terrible today. In any case, I must be going. One last thing, Mrs. Godwin—you wouldn't happen to be a . . . Custodian, would you?"

"Custodian?" Mrs. Godwin looked puzzled. "No. Why do you ask?"

"Oh, dear. That is unfortunate. Well, good day, Mrs. Godwin." He bowed. "And to you too, Master Godwin."

Mrs. Godwin smiled. "Good day to you too."

After Mr. Benjamin left, Victor locked the door. "How could you do that?"

"Do what, Victor?"

Victor marched over to the table by the door. He picked up a three-ring binder and thumped it with his forefinger.

"Don't you remember? The fifteen-point plan I assembled for you to find the perfect tenant?" He opened the binder and began to recite: "Step One: Questionnaire; Step Two: Background Check; Step Three: Three-Day Waiting Period; Step Four—"

"Step Four, listen to your mother." Mrs. Godwin took the binder from Victor's hand. "I appreciate the work you put into this, sweetie, but it's been months. No one else seems to want the place, and we need the money. Besides, he looks like he's an honest man."

"He looks like Benjamin Franklin, Mom. I mean, who dresses like that when they're trying to rent an apartment?"

"He explained that to me before you came downstairs. He's an actor and he's on his way to rehearsal." Mrs. Godwin raised an eyebrow at Victor. "Besides, *you're* one to talk about how other people dress."

"That's different," Victor explained. "Wearing the same thing every day increases my efficiency by—"

"Victor, he paid an entire year's rent in advance—in

gold!" Mrs. Godwin reached into her sweater pocket and pulled out a small handful of coins. "They look like antiques."

Victor examined one of the gold coins. He was surprised at how heavy it felt. A man's face was engraved on the front, encircled by some Latin words and the year 1783. It looked and felt genuine.

"Probably fake," Victor said. "It's not too late to tell Mr. Benjamin that this was a mistake. Let's stick with my plan. According to my research, it has a 98 percent chance of detecting a well-paid, dependable, *normal* tenant."

"Knowing you, that may be so." Mrs. Godwin took back the coin. "But for now, we're going with my plan, which I am calling the We-Need-the-Money-So-Mr.-Benjamin-Is-Moving-In Plan."

Sometimes, Victor didn't understand his mother at all.

---

4 ESCUDO GOLD COIN (SPANISH, *1783*)

CHAPTER FOUR

A Mysterious Noise

A week passed, and Victor had to admit that his mother had been at least a little bit right. Mr. Benjamin was a pretty quiet tenant, and he kept to himself.

The gold coins had turned out to be genuine too. The money Mrs. Godwin received from selling them was enough to cover the downstairs rent for a year. She was even starting to talk about them taking a vacation someday.

Still, there was something about Mr. Benjamin that Victor didn't trust. Where had he come from? Why hadn't he brought any references? And even if he was an actor, what kind of a man paid for things in eighteenth-century Spanish doubloons?

Too many questions. Once the science fair was over,

there would be time to figure it all out. But right now, Victor had a serious problem to fix.

His graph was the wrong color.

It had come to him last night in his sleep. More than 60 percent of the winning projects had used red and blue lines. Victor, foolishly, had drawn his in red and green. The only solution would be to make a new one from scratch. And with less than a week before the fair, he'd have to work fast.

He spread out the paper on his desk and measured the border with a long ruler. With great care, he began to sketch a line along the edge.

BANG!

The sound came from downstairs. Mr. Benjamin, it seemed, was home.

POW!

Victor's pencil slipped off the ruler, ruining his line. How was he supposed to get any work done with all that noise?

BANG! POW! URP! KA-POW!

This was ridiculous. Gold coins or not, Mr. Benjamin had no right to make such a racket on a Sunday morning. As soon as his mom got home, he would ask her to—

BANG! BANG! BANG! BANG! BANG! URP.

Victor threw down his pencil and stormed out to the hall. "Mr. Benjamin! I'm trying to work up here. Can you keep it down?"

Grrrrrrrrrrp. POW!

"Mr. Benjamin! It's very important that I finish this graph."

· BANG!

Enough was enough. Victor stomped down the stairs and pounded on Mr. Benjamin's apartment door. There was no reply, so he knocked again, harder. The door creaked open.

"Mr. Benjamin? It's Victor, from upstairs." He poked his head inside.

It looked as if no one had ever moved in. The apartment was completely, 100 percent empty. There was no furniture or carpeting, and there were no pictures on the walls.

It didn't make sense. Why would someone go to all the expense of renting an apartment if he wasn't going to use it?

Cautiously, Victor stepped inside. "Mr. Benjamin?"

KA-BANG!

The sound echoed through the open rooms. From what he could tell, it had come from the living room. Victor tiptoed over and peered around the corner.

That room, like the others, was bare, except for a set of tall bookshelves built into the wall. It was strange to see them so empty. When Mr. Mercer had been alive, those shelves had been crammed full of strange old books.

Because Mr. Mercer had had no family to claim his belongings, it had been up to Victor and his mom to figure out what to do with them. They sold most of the

PROPER TOOLS AND SUPPLIES FOR CUSTODIANS

Without the proper tools, a custodian is nothing more than a man in a jumpsuit. On the right you will find a list of the best equipment at the best prices. *The Custodian's Guide to Maintaining Your Mop* recommends tools found only at C.I. Pherkey Custodial and Cleaning Supplies, Inc. For quality in cleaning, accept no substitutes.

Ordering information can be found in Appendix C.

Obscuring Paste (O-13)

TOOL	MODEL #	COST
Basic Mop	A-14	$2.99
Extra-wide Mop	B-21	$3.99
Waterproof Mop Oil	C-4	$0.99
Aluminum Mop Bucket	D-9	$2.99
Reinforced Mop Bucket	E-3	$3.99
Edging Brush	F-1	$0.89
Two-sided Edging Brush	G-25	$1.19
Hand-held Desk Brush	H-18	$0.89
Epoxy Putty	I-12	$0.39
Electric Bristle Broom	J-7	$7.49
Magnetic Bristle Broom	K-17	$5.49
Plastic Bristle Broom	L-10	$1.99
Extra Bristles (1 box)	M-8	$0.39
Repairing Paste (1 gal.)	N-15	$1.29
Obscuring Paste (1 gal.)	O-13	$1.29
Rubber Gloves (10 pair)	P-24	$0.49
Hand Soap (1 qt.)	Q-23	$0.59
Erasing Pads (4 pack)	R-16	$0.89
Hinge Oil	S-11	$0.49
Electric Hinge Oil	T-20	$0.59
Anti-Graffiti Spray	U-6	$1.19
Razor Knife	V-5	$0.49
Sanitary Jumpsuit	W-22	$12.99
Antiseptic Boots	X-26	$5.99
Laminated Name Patch	Y-2	$0.79
Linen Handkerchiefs	Z-19	$0.39

The Custodian's Guide to Maintaining Your Mop
23

Excerpt from
The Custodian's Guide to Maintaining Your Mop
(1957 Edition)

books to an auction house, but Victor had claimed a few of the more unusual titles for himself: *Electricity and the Circulatory System, Brain Wave Amplification of the Ether,* and *The Custodian's Guide to Maintaining Your Mop—1957 Edition.* One of these days, he planned to read them.

As he gazed at the empty shelves, Victor noticed something odd. One of the bookcases had been pulled a few inches from the wall.

Victor crept closer, his heart pounding.

He tugged at the shelf and it swung open like a door. Behind it, Victor could see a dark, narrow shaft. A wooden ladder clamped to one wall led downward, and an eerie blue glow shined from somewhere far below. Cool, musty air filled his nostrils.

Victor knelt down and peeked over the edge. At the bottom of the shaft, about ten feet down, he could see a dusty floor and the curved edge of a large room. Several strange machines lined the wall, and long shadows flickered in the blue light.

Brblbrblbrblb-BOOM!

There was a bright electric flash, followed by the faint smell of something burning.

Mr. Benjamin—if that was even his real name—was up to something. Had he known about this secret passage when he rented the house? Had he lied to Victor and his mom? Now he was down there doing who knows what. Building a bomb, probably.

This was exactly why Victor had prepared the fifteen-point tenant approval plan.

Victor's mind raced. What should he do first? Call his mom? Or the police?

Both. But first, he needed proof. Victor pulled his cell phone from his pocket and switched on the camera.

With a deep breath, he reached for the ladder. As lightly as he could, he placed one foot, then the next, onto the wooden rungs. He wouldn't go far. Just low enough to peek under the—

Suddenly, the wood beneath his feet cracked. Victor's foot shot downward. He clutched at the rung above. That broke, too, as the entire ladder split in half.

Victor plummeted to the floor below.

CHAPTER FIVE

A Shocking Surprise

It was as if Victor had fallen into the guts of an enormous machine. Rusty gears, pulleys, and pipes crisscrossed a shadowy, candlelit room. Three workbenches stood piled high with old tools. Glass jars lined the stone walls, and something inside made them glow, bathing the room in an eerie blue light. They reminded Victor of Leyden jars, a kind of old-fashioned battery from the 1700s. He had built one once, as an experiment. But his hadn't looked like these.

And then Victor saw him.

"Mr. Benjamin!" Victor cried. "Are you okay?"

In the center of the room, the old man lay across a large steel and glass box, his body convulsing. Wires stretched from his collar up to a giant metal orb, which hung from the ceiling. It emitted a deep, pulsating hum—a tone so low, Victor could feel it vibrating in his bones. Mr. Benjamin was clutching a cable with a brass cone at the end. Sparks danced from his fingertips up his arm to his head. White smoke streamed from his ears. The air smelled like melting plastic.

Victor scanned the room. He spotted an old mop with a wooden handle leaning against a workbench. Wood was an insulator. It would keep him from being electrocuted.

He grabbed the mop, held it like a lance, and charged toward the old man. Taking a mighty swing, he knocked the brass cone from Mr. Benjamin's hands. The sparks died, and the orb's eerie humming ceased.

Mr. Benjamin lay still. Victor cautiously reached toward the old man's neck to feel for a pulse. As he did, a tremendous shock raced up Victor's arm, throwing him back against the wall. Mr. Benjamin sprang to his feet, his eyes glowing bright.

"Long live the Modern Order of Prometheus!"

The old man stumbled back against a workbench and shook his head. He looked like he had just awakened from a bad dream.

THE STANDARD CUSTODIAN'S MOP

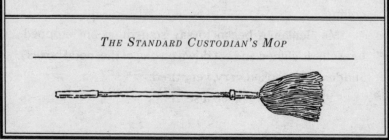

"Are you . . . a Promethean?" The voice was groggy and low.

Victor froze.

"Young man! Why have I been awakened? Are you a Promethean?"

"I'm . . . uh, Victor? From upstairs?"

Mr. Benjamin tilted his head, confused. "You're not from the Order?"

"The Order?"

"The Modern Order of—" Mr. Benjamin paused. His ears had stopped smoking and his eyes were no longer glowing. "Ah yes, Victor. From upstairs."

"Are you okay? It looked like your head was on fire."

"It appears my electrophone was not properly grounded. I must have been caught in an electrical feedback loop." Mr. Benjamin ran his fingers through his stringy hair and under his collar.

Victor gasped. "What are those things on your neck?"

Immediately, Mr. Benjamin yanked his collar back up.

"And those wires coming out of your shirt? That giant metal ball up there? And that big glass box—is that a coffin?"

Mr. Benjamin began to say something but stopped himself. He sighed and sat down on one of the metal boxes. Suddenly, he looked very, very tired.

"Victor, can you keep a secret?"

CHAPTER SIX

The Modern Order of Prometheus

"*First of all,* my name is not Frank Benjamin. It is . . . *Benjamin Franklin.*"

Victor snorted. "Sure you are. And I'm Albert Einstein."

"Albert? I thought your name was Victor."

Victor shook his head. "I was being sarcastic. Everyone knows Benjamin Franklin has been dead for more than two hundred years."

"Not dead, Victor. Just sleeping."

Victor backed away. "Look, Mr. Benjamin, I think the electricity must have—"

"Hear me out, Victor. I *am* Benjamin Franklin, and I can prove it." The old man pulled a candle from its holder. Its flame flickered. "Victor, do you know the story of Prometheus?"

"Uh, it's a Greek myth," Victor said. "Prometheus stole the secret of fire from the gods and gave it to mankind."

"Exactly. And this fire allowed mankind to stay warm, to cook food, and to forge metal. In that fire, science itself was born. It was the greatest gift civilization had ever received."

The old man lifted the candle to his face and studied the flame. For a moment, he was lost in thought.

"But fire was not the only secret that the gods had withheld from mankind. There was another, even greater secret."

He handed Victor the candle.

"I remember how it all began. I had been performing several crude experiments in electricity."

"Like flying a kite in a thunderstorm."

The old man smiled. "You know of that?"

"Of course. The kite, the key . . ."

"Yes! That experiment proved that lightning was electricity. I was even able to store the charge inside a Leyden jar."

Victor glanced at the glowing blue cylinders circling the room. So they *were* Leyden jars after all.

"Some time later, I was contacted by a French scientist named Dubourg. He theorized that the human body is a natural Leyden jar. People are born with a full battery of life energy. As they live their lives, they use that energy little by little. Finally, when their batteries have completely emptied, they die."

With a flourish, the old man blew out the candle flame.

"Ah, but what if one could recharge the battery of life? Mankind could cheat death itself! That, Victor, was the secret the gods had dangled just out of our reach—*immortality*! And so, my lad, we created the Modern Order of Prometheus!"

He sprang to his feet and began to pace. Blue sparks shot from the tangle of wires running to metal bolts in his neck. Around the room, the Leyden jars began to pulsate. Victor took a step back.

"After years of failure, we were close. We couldn't stop death entirely, but we believed we could suspend life indefinitely. I was eighty-four years old and dying. By my estimate, I had less than a month to live. My body's battery was nearly empty, so I volunteered to be the first. If the process proved successful, other scientists would follow.

"The Prometheans would awaken me in the distant future, at a time of great emergency when civilization needed me most. Until that time, I would hibernate. But there was great risk."

"Risk?" said Victor.

"Explosion! Electrocution! Jefferson thought I would turn into a raisin, soaking in the liquid for so long." He chuckled. "Of course, some would say I was a bit of a raisin before I climbed in!"

Victor shook his head. "So what's this great emergency? Who woke you up?"

The old man shook his head. "I was hoping you might know. My life battery drains as we speak. I fear I have only weeks to discover the crisis *and* attend to it. Time is of the essence!"

Victor ran a finger across the thick layer of dust on the table. It was all too fantastic to believe. Yet the evidence was all there: the hidden laboratory, the antique technology—and he *did* look a lot like Benjamin Franklin. But his story was impossible. Wasn't it?

"So how did all this work, exactly?" Victor asked.

"In this very laboratory, I climbed into the Leyden casket." The old man gestured to the glass and metal coffin in the middle of the room. "My loyal assistant—a Custodian—sealed the lid, pulled the lever, and sent me into my deep hibernation."

THE LEYDEN CASKET

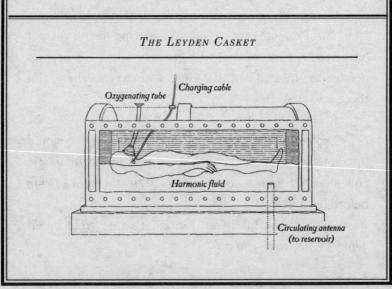

Oxygenating tube

Charging cable

Harmonic fluid

Circulating antenna
(to reservoir)

"Custodian?" Victor asked. "Like the people who clean schools?"

"My boy, Custodians can do anything!" the old man said. "But as a Promethean, his main duty—and that of his descendants—was to oversee the experiment until I awoke. The lightning attractor on the chimney supplied a constant stream of electricity to the Leyden jars. This electricity kept me just barely alive in suspended animation for centuries."

Victor leaned in closer. "What was it like?"

"It was as if no time had passed at all. A brief nap. When I awoke, I assumed there would be a great problem for me to solve. Unfortunately, it appears that something has gone very wrong. My Custodian is nowhere to be found, and my remaining power is dwindling."

"Mr. Mercer was a custodian," Victor said. "He had the apartment before you."

"Excellent! Where can I find him? I must speak with him immediately."

"You can't. Mr. Mercer died months ago."

The old man's face darkened. "Oh, dear. How did it happen?"

"Heart attack," Victor said. "But he couldn't have been one of your Custodians. He was just a regular janitor. I think he worked at the high school or something."

Franklin sighed. "This may be worse than I thought. Now it is even more urgent that I contact the other Prometheans. Only they know what I must do." He gestured to the strange brass cone Victor had knocked from his hands. "But to contact them, I must repair the electrophone before time runs out."

The old man sat down. For a moment, neither of them spoke.

"I'm sorry, Mr. Benjamin, but—"

"Call me Ben."

"Okay, Ben, this . . . this is all a bit, well, crazy. You want me to believe that you're the real Benjamin Franklin, you're hundreds of years old, and you run on electricity?"

The old man chuckled. "When you put it that way, it does sound a bit preposterous." He thought for a moment and snapped his fingers. "Perhaps *this* will convince you that the flame of life can be rekindled."

He clutched his stomach, tipped his head, and let rip a thunderous burp.

Brrrrrrrrr-BANG!

Sparks flew from his mouth and exploded in front of his face. His eyes glowed bright blue. The smell of fireworks filled the air.

Victor jumped back, stunned. He gazed in astonishment at the candle in his hand. It had reignited and was burning even brighter than before!

Benjamin Franklin rubbed his stomach. "It seems that sleeping for two hundred years has given me quite a case of gas."

CHAPTER SEVEN
Hunger!

Victor was having a hard time wrapping his brain around the idea.

Only a few hours ago, he had discovered one of the Founding Fathers in his basement. Now, the two of them were up on the roof watching the sun setting over the city.

"There's got to be someone else who can help you," Victor said. "The police? The president? What about the Franklin Institute?"

"I have an institute?" Franklin said. "Fascinating! But no, only the Prometheans must know of my existence in your century. Until we can determine the nature of the great emergency, we dare not trust anyone else. Secrecy is essential."

Together, they examined a strange iron contraption attached to the rod on the chimney. Years of rain and wind had taken their toll, and a thick layer of rust covered every surface. Victor pried open the casing with a screwdriver. Inside, he found a confusing tangle of frayed wires, tarnished silver plates, and rusty bolts.

"It doesn't make sense," said Franklin. "It looks as if no one has maintained this part of the electrophone in fifty years."

"What is it supposed to do?"

"It sends my voice in a burst of invisible Hyperion waves across the ether. At the other end, the Prometheans will hear my call with their magnetic signal catchers. They can respond in the same way."

Victor nodded. "So it's a type of radio. The rod on the chimney is your antenna. And this box must be some sort of transceiver."

"Transceiver?" said Franklin. "Radio?"

"That's right," said Victor. "The copper cone in the basement is probably a microphone. I bet the signal is broadcast through the metal rods up here, along the chimney." He examined two of the silver plates in the box. "But if it were me, I'd widen the gaps between these plates. It would double the signal strength."

The old man let out a long, hearty laugh. "Victor, I am fortunate to have found you. Please hand me that hammer."

Franklin took the hammer from Victor's hands and began banging on the plates inside the box.

"Whoa!" Victor shouted, grabbing Franklin's arm. "What are you doing? You'll break it!"

"Nonsense, my boy. I've been working on electrophones since before you were born. A few more taps should do it."

"Just slow down," Victor sputtered. "Instead of just hitting things with a hammer, we need to proceed scientifically, to make sure we don't cause further damage. That takes time."

"Time?" Franklin chuckled. "Victor, that's the one thing I don't have. True, the scientific method has its place in an ideal situation, but my situation is less than ideal. For now, we'll have to trust our instincts, whack away at the problem, and hope for the best."

Victor frowned. "The last time you ignored the proper measuring and testing, you ended up short-circuiting yourself in the basement."

"Ah, but if I hadn't short-circuited myself, you would never have rescued me, and I wouldn't have your keen scientific mind to help guide me now."

"But—"

"No buts! Time is of the essence," Franklin said, peering over his bifocals at the device. "There! That should hold. But it appears many modifications have been made to the electrophone since my day. Perhaps you can help me divine where these wires are supposed to go."

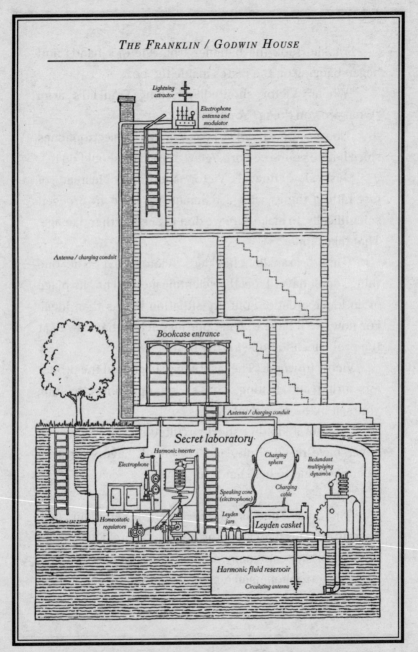

Lightning attractor

Electrophone antenna and modulator

Antenna / charging conduit

Bookcase entrance

Antenna / charging conduit

Secret laboratory

Harmonic inverter

Electrophone

Charging sphere

Redundant multiplying dynamos

Charging cable

Speaking cone (electrophone)

Leyden jars

Homeostatic regulators

Leyden casket

Harmonic fluid reservoir

Circulating antenna

Before long, they had repaired the worst of it. It wasn't pretty, but it would do.

"This antenna, it's also your lightning attractor?" said Victor, wrapping the base with an extra layer of duct tape.

"Exactly," Franklin said. "While I slept, the lightning attractor collected electricity from the air. That energy was used to recharge the Leyden jars. Those Leyden jars charged me, keeping me alive during my hibernation."

Thunder rumbled in the distance. Victor felt a few raindrops on the back of his neck.

"Ben, you told me that you have only a month left to live. If the Leyden jars kept you alive all that time, couldn't we just hook you up to them again and keep you going?"

Franklin didn't answer. He was frozen, staring into space.

"Ben? Hello?"

Franklin shook his head. "I'm sorry. I was . . . what was the question? Ah, yes. The Leyden jars. Unfortunately, they were only powerful enough to sustain me during suspended animation. Now that I've awakened, I'm afraid . . . I'm afraid that . . ."

"Are you all right?"

"I'm sorry," Franklin said, squeezing his eyes shut and then opening them again. "I'm suddenly feeling a bit run down, like a clock that needs winding. I'll be fine."

The rain fell, light but steady. Together, Victor and Franklin watched the city lights blink on, one by one.

"I imagine Philadelphia looks quite a bit different from your day," said Victor.

The old man smiled. "It is breathtaking. Buildings so tall, they seem to pierce the sky, and wagons that travel without horse or ox—astonishing!"

Victor's stomach growled. He reached into his pocket and pulled out a snack. "Do you want some? It's called a Frootbär. It's like fruit, only better."

Franklin tore off a small piece and tasted it. He made a sour face and spat it out. "What is it? Some sort of shoe leather?"

"I've got Gummy-Raisins too." Victor held out a small bag of bright blue nuggets.

"Thank you, no. I have little appetite for food just now. I need . . . what do I need?" Franklin gazed at a power cable that stretched from a utility pole to the Godwins' rooftop. "I need . . ."

"Ben, are you okay? You look pale."

Franklin rose to his feet and lumbered, trancelike, to the cable.

"Don't touch that," Victor warned. "It's not safe."

"Hungry," whispered Franklin. "So hungry . . ."

He picked up the cable and studied it in his hands. His eyes grew wide and his bolts crackled. Impulsively, he brought it to his mouth and took a bite, grinding his teeth through the plastic insulation to the charged wires at its center.

ZZZZZZZZZAP!

Franklin roared, his body jerking and vibrating. Sparks spun off his molars, and his eyes glowed bright red. His hair stood on end, and his whole body was surrounded in a blue, pulsating aura.

Victor recoiled, falling back against the chimney.

What was happening to Ben?

He was wild, stumbling back and forth like a monster, his face savage and fierce.

"Ben?"

Franklin ground his teeth on the cable until it stopped sparking. The lights on the east side of Victor's neighborhood flickered. Block by block, they went dark.

The old man threw the cable down and turned west.

"MORE!"

ABOUT LIGHTNING

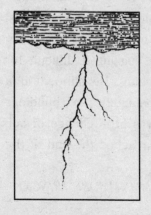

Lightning strikes can reach a temperature of 50,000 degrees Fahrenheit and can contain 100 million volts of electricity. In a given year, the Earth is home to approximately 16 million thunderstorms, 1,800 of which are happening at this very minute.

Source: National Weather Service

CHAPTER EIGHT
Franklinstein Walks the Earth!

Like a missile locked onto its target, Franklin charged across the rooftop. His head was tipped to the side, and blue drool dripped from the corner of his mouth. He held his arms outstretched, as if reaching for something.

Victor raced after him. The old man leaped onto Mrs. Vamos's roof. "Ben, hold on! Wait for me!"

The rain beat down harder, making it difficult for Victor to see where he was going. He slipped in a puddle but caught himself. Thankfully, the buildings were close enough that there was little chance of falling into an alley. But once they reached the end of the block . . .

Franklin surged on faster. *"MMMMMMORE! HUNGRY!"*

Victor pumped his arms and legs harder and gained some ground.

By the time he caught up, Franklin had reached the last rooftop.

"Ben, you have to stop!" Victor screamed. "You'll fall!"

One inch from the edge, Franklin came to a dead stop. He swiveled his head, sniffing the air like a bloodhound on the trail. Lightning flashed, and for a moment Franklin glowed even brighter.

Victor steadied himself, hunched over, his hands on his knees, and tried to catch his breath. "Ben," he huffed. "What's happening to you?"

Franklin turned his head and looked blankly at Victor. Victor looked on in horror as Franklin bent his knees and leapt straight out, off the edge.

"Ben!" Victor heard a loud crack on the sidewalk below. He flattened his belly against the rooftop, grabbed on to the gutters with his fingers, and peered over the edge.

But Franklin wasn't there. Only a large, crooked crack in the sidewalk . . . *on the other side of the street!*

He spied Franklin halfway up a utility pole. The electricity from one side of town hadn't been enough. He wanted . . .

"MORE!"

Thunder cracked. Victor clambered down the fire

escape and ran across the street. Forty feet up, Franklin hung from the top of the pole, his left hand clutching another power cable. He thrashed from side to side in a spasmodic electric dance. Energy surged through his body and sparks crackled off his toes. He glowed so bright that Victor had to squint.

Rain poured down harder. Franklin reached an arm into the storming sky, as if trying to wrench lightning from the clouds.

BOOM!

Suddenly, the sky flashed white with a crack of thunder so loud that Victor's ears rang. A bolt of lightning zagged down from the clouds, striking Franklin in the chest. The old man plunged to the sidewalk.

Victor ran over to Franklin and knelt down. The old man lay unmoving on the pavement, his eyes closed. A low hum emanated from somewhere deep inside Franklin's body.

"Ben?" Slowly, Victor reached out a hand.

ZAP!

A violent shock of electricity shot through the air and up Victor's arm, throwing him back into the gutter.

The crackling electricity continued to dance and snap in the air around Franklin's body. The old man shook, sparks flying from his neck bolts. His foot touched a lamppost, and a great arc of energy shot up the pole, exploding the bulb with a flash.

Franklin sprang to his feet. His whole body vibrated and his eyes rolled in his head. He glowed like a neon sign. It was almost as if he had more energy than he knew what to do with.

Victor took a step back. Was he going to explode?

Thunder pounded. Franklin ran.

Victor raced behind as Franklin rampaged blindly through a series of backyards, with no apparent sense of direction or purpose. He crushed a swing set and flattened a barbecue grill. After circling a swimming pool, he came to a wooden fence and paused, confused.

Victor caught up. "Ben, we need to get you back to the lab."

Franklin swung a mighty arm, smashed the fence to splinters, and charged into the next backyard.

Victor ran after him through the hole in the fence, then through holes in three other fences in three other backyards.

His lungs burned, and he paused to catch his breath. Was chasing Ben even a good idea? After all, he was dangerous. He had given Victor quite a nasty shock. Victor could have been killed.

But he was *Benjamin Franklin*. And he was confused. Victor could see it on his face. He had to help, for the old man's sake. For history's sake. And for the sake of anyone who might get in his way.

Victor heard a scream.

He dashed down the street and through an alley, following the sounds to Pirate Pete's Fish Fry. Its entire front plate-glass window had been smashed in, and debris littered the sidewalk. Victor raced inside. Fish sandwiches were strewn about the floor. A soda machine, tipped on its side, sprayed orange soda into the air. A man in a pirate costume peeked up from behind the cash register.

"Which way did he go?" Victor asked.

With a trembling hook, the pirate gestured toward the back of the restaurant.

"Thanks!" Victor ran past the deep fryers out the back door, which was hanging by a single hinge.

Across the street, Victor spotted Franklin barreling into the park toward the big fountain. He took a deep breath and ran after him.

"Ben!" Victor screamed. "Wait up!"

Franklin ignored him and leaped into the water.

FWOOOSH!

Instantly, the water vaporized, enveloping Franklin in a thick cloud of steam. By the time Victor caught up, the steam had cleared and the old man had vanished.

For an hour, Victor searched frantically. Evidence of Franklin's rampage was scattered throughout the neighborhood. A Dumpster turned on its end. A fire hydrant ripped from the sidewalk, spewing water into the sky.

But Franklin himself was nowhere to be found.

CHAPTER NINE
Aftermath

By eleven o'clock, the power had returned. Victor sat glued to his computer, watching the online news reports trickle in. City officials were blaming the outage on a large animal that had chewed through a power cable. A woman from Animal Control urged residents to remain calm and keep their doors and windows locked. Evidently the animal, which some reports were calling a bear, had climbed a utility pole as well. She expressed confidence that it would be caught by morning.

Meanwhile, not far away, a crazed intruder had gone berserk in a fast-food restaurant, causing thousands of dollars in damage. Police were investigating.

Finally, authorities reported that all the water from

a fountain in a local park had mysteriously vanished.

To Victor's relief, there was no mention of Benjamin Franklin.

So where *was* he? It wasn't like Franklin knew anyone in modern-day Philadelphia except for that organization he had mentioned. What was it called? Something about Prometheus . . .

Victor typed *Modern Order of Prometheus* into the search box. There were over a million hits, and all of them had something to do with the famous monster novel *Frankenstein*. To Victor's surprise, the subtitle of that book was actually *The Modern Prometheus*. Victor wondered what Franklin would make of that coincidence.

There was even an online store called Modern Prometheus Books. A list of titles ran down the page: *Frankenstein's Monster in Movies*; *Movie Makeup Secrets of Frankenstein*; *The Frankenstein Legend*; *Mary Shelley: A Biography*. Every book was about Frankenstein except one: *The Custodian's Guide to Maintaining Your Mop*.

THE SEAL OF THE MODERN ORDER OF PROMETHEUS

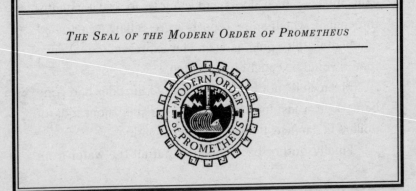

Benjamin Franklinstein Lives!

Why did that title sound so familiar? He clicked on the picture of the book, but nothing happened. Another dead end.

Six hours later, Victor checked his watch and cursed. He had been up all night searching the Web and was no closer to finding Ben. Plus, he was late for the bus. He shut down his computer, threw on his Monday clothes, and grabbed his umbrella. It was going to be a long day.

By the time he arrived at the bus stop, Scott Weaver was already there, hunched over his backpack, struggling to keep his books dry.

"Hey, Victor," said Scott. "This is funny, huh? I'm on time, and you're the one who's late."

Victor winced.

"Up all night working on your science project? I bet yours is going to be awesome." Scott shivered. "Can I stand under your umbrella?"

Victor made room and Scott shuffled over. "Thanks," he said. "No one at my house remembered to check the weather."

The sky above was charcoal gray. Beneath them, a river of rainwater poured into the gutter.

"Did you hear about the bear?" said Scott. "My dad says it's just a publicity stunt. You know, for a movie or something."

Thunder rumbled from somewhere far away, and Victor thought of Franklin. Was he okay?

"Something special's going to happen in science class today," said Scott. "Want to know what it is?"

"Okay."

"I can't tell you. It's a surprise. Also, I'm making another potato battery to enter in the science fair. This one's going to be even better."

Victor sighed. A potato battery was a sucker bet. Statistics showed it had a less than 3 percent chance of winning. If it didn't explode.

"I figured out the problem with the last one," Scott continued. "I wasn't supposed to put batteries inside it. The potato *is* the battery. Cool, huh?"

Victor rubbed his eyes. He was half asleep. And the half that was awake felt like it was in a dream.

"Victor, are you okay?"

"Sorry, Scott. It sounds great. Really."

"That's what I thought. Tonight, I'm going out to the shed to look for more cool stuff to stick in the potato. But not batteries. The principal said I'm not allowed to do that anymore. Want to help?"

"You mean you haven't even started? But the science fair is Friday."

Scott shrugged. "I know. But that last potato was pretty neat. Maybe I'll get lucky again."

"Science isn't about luck, Scott." Victor felt his jaw tighten. "And your last potato wasn't neat, it was dangerous. You could have started a fire."

"I did start a fire," said Scott, holding up his hand. "That's why my fingernails turned black. Don't you remember?"

"But that's not what the science fair is about," said Victor. "You're just messing around with stuff, hoping something happens."

"I know. My dad told me that's how Alexander Gramble invented the telephone. He spilled something on it."

"Alexander *Graham Bell*. Besides, that doesn't count because . . . because . . ." Victor was almost shouting now. "It's complicated. A potato battery is a stupid project. It won't win, Scott."

Scott's face fell. "My dad thought my potato was awesome." He tucked his books into his jacket and stepped out from under the umbrella.

For a minute, they stood in silence, watching the rain fall. Victor sighed. "Sorry."

"I hope you win, Victor. It sounds like it means a lot to you."

ALEXANDER GRAHAM BELL EXPERIMENTING WITH THE
POTATO-POWERED TELEPHONE, 1879

CHAPTER TEN
The Return of Franklinstein!

The school day dragged on, and Victor found it impossible to concentrate. He had developed a nervous spasm in his stomach that wouldn't go away. When his social studies teacher, Mrs. Engel, mentioned the Franklin stove, Victor nearly threw up. He ran to the bathroom and hid in a stall for the rest of the period.

At least he could end the day on an easy note. Science was his last class, and his volcano was in solid shape. While everyone else was working on their projects, Victor would have a chance to collect his thoughts.

"All right, everyone, settle down." Mr. Bohr's voice sounded strangely giddy. "We've got a special guest today, a bit of a science celebrity."

Across the aisle, Scott winked at Victor.

"I'm sure you all know Skip Weaver, meteorologist with our local station WURP." He opened the door and Skip Weaver came bounding into the room, cameraman in tow. Skip was wearing a rain jacket and a pillowy foam hat shaped like a big thundercloud.

Victor groaned. So this was Scott's big surprise.

"Hiya, kids!" said Skip, beaming. "Anyone know the worst thing about being a weatherman?"

Angela Willbrant raised her hand but, as usual, didn't wait to be called on. "Mr. Bohr, does this mean we're going to be on TV?"

"You'll have to ask Mr. Weaver," said Mr. Bohr, gesturing politely to his guest.

"That's why I'm here," said Skip. "Now, who knows the worst part about being a weatherman?"

Denny Burkus raised his hand. "Do that thing where you make your stomach talk!" Several other kids hollered in agreement.

"Can do," said Skip. "But first, listen—the worst thing is that, if I do my job wrong . . ."

He squeezed something inside his jacket pocket, and water poured down from the cloud on his head.

"*. . . I'm all wet!*"

The class cheered.

Mr. Bohr cleared his throat. "That's, uh, very interesting. Now, class, I've asked Mr. Weaver here to talk to you about what it means to be a real scientist. We all know he's a very entertaining fellow, but I'm sure you must have some serious scientific questions you'd like to ask. Anyone? Yes, Dylan?"

"Is it hard being a real scientist?" asked Dylan Parsons.

"Not at all," said Skip. "In fact, you could say . . ."

He pressed another button and a speaker in his hat rumbled like thunder.

"*. . . it's a blast!*"

Victor's stomach churned. Real scientist? Skip Weaver was no more a real scientist than a monkey in a lab coat. No, scratch that. At least the monkey looked the part. Victor closed his eyes, took a deep breath, and tried to think calm thoughts. Robots. Integrated circuits. The Pythagorean theorem. Anything but Skip Weaver or—

"*Benjamin Franklin!*"

Victor's eyes shot open. For some reason, everyone was staring out the window behind him. He spun around.

There, tapping on the glass, was Franklin. He looked terrible. His blue glow was gone, and his skin was dusty gray. His lids hung low over his eyes. He was drooling.

"*Victorrrrr . . .*"

Angela Willbrant screamed.

"It's okay, everyone!" said Victor, jumping to his feet. "He's . . . my uncle."

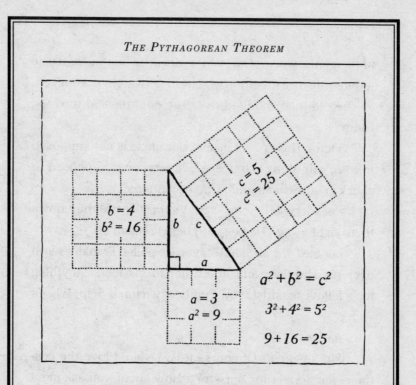

"Is he feeling okay?" asked Mr. Bohr. "Why is he dressed like Benjamin Franklin?"

"Vic-torrrrr . . ."

"It's, uh, his job," said Victor. "He must be on break." He pulled open the window and lowered his head.

"Ben!" he whispered. "Are you all right? Where have you been? You need to get home."

"Victorrrr!" Franklin's eyes flashed in recognition. He lunged toward Victor and began to pull himself through the window.

"Ben, no!" hissed Victor, but it was too late. Franklin's

movements were slow and awkward, but he had the momentum of a locomotive. The class watched, shocked, as the old man tumbled over the counter and into the room.

"Victor, this is . . . I mean your uncle is not supposed to . . . ," Mr. Bohr stammered. "Everyone is supposed to check in at the main office, no exceptions!"

"I'm sorry, Mr. Bohr," said Victor. "I'll take him down there right away." He began to help Franklin up.

"Let me." It was Skip Weaver. He pulled Franklin's arm over his shoulder and lifted him to his feet. "Anything for a fellow scientist. Say, buddy, my name's Skip. What's yours?"

"Bennnn . . ."

Skip laughed. "Of course it is. Listen, I love the costume. It's perfect for our story. How about you ask me a few questions about science, with all the kids gathered around? At the end, you can pretend to fly a kite under my hat. It'll be a hoot."

"Mr. Weaver, I'm afraid my uncle won't be able to—"

"Nonsense, kid, it'll be great." He gestured to the cameraman. "Jim, can we get this guy a microphone?"

Franklin looked utterly confused.

Victor felt panic rise through his body. He still had no idea what to do about Franklin, but putting him on the evening news was certainly not the answer. He needed help. A distraction.

He needed Scott Weaver.

"Hey, Scott. Your new potato battery—is it ready to go?"

"Just about," said Scott. He held up a lumpy, tape-wrapped ball about the size of a grapefruit. It was dripping a strange black liquid.

"Can we try it out? You know, to see if it works?"

Scott shrugged. "I don't know. It's not quite done. I was thinking maybe some ketchup . . ."

"They're about to roll." Victor gestured toward the camera. "It would be great for the broadcast."

Scott held the potato at arm's length. The black liquid dripped down his sleeve. "I guess so. It's about to

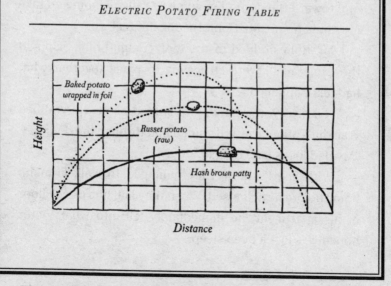

ELECTRIC POTATO FIRING TABLE

Height

Baked potato wrapped in foil

Russet potato (raw)

Hash brown patty

Distance

fall apart anyway." He set it down on his desk and began to unwind two wires.

At the front of the room, Franklin tottered back and forth as the cameraman tried to line up the shot. The rest of the students watched in fascination. Mr. Bohr looked very concerned.

"See, the way I figure it," said Scott, "if I just connect these two wires, it should—"

Spla-BOOOOM!

The potato took off across the room like a giant rocket-propelled spitball. It narrowly missed Mr. Bohr's nose and struck the cameraman squarely on the side of the head. He toppled to the floor. Skip Weaver raced to his side. Angela Willbrant screamed.

Victor ran to Franklin and grabbed his wrist, yanking him toward the door. "I'm going to call my mom and take my uncle home, Mr. Bohr. He doesn't feel well."

Mr. Bohr nodded distractedly. Behind him, Skip and the cameraman were struggling to piece together what had just happened.

"I'll give you a hand," whispered Scott. He grabbed Franklin's other arm and guided him through the doorway. "My dad looks kind of mad."

With Scott's help, they managed to walk Franklin home before he collapsed. When they laid him on the floor of his apartment, he immediately fell into what Victor hoped was just a deep sleep.

"Is this where he lives?" Scott asked. "Where's his furniture and stuff?"

"He just moved in," Victor said.

"He smells like a cave. Is he sick?"

"Look, Scott," said Victor, "he's going to be just fine. I told you, my uncle Frank just gets like this sometimes. Thanks again for your help."

"No problem," said Scott.

"Shouldn't you be going?"

"That's okay. I can stay. You know, in case you need me."

Victor sighed. He had enough on his plate right now without Scott looking over his shoulder. If only he knew whom he could go to for help.

"Hey, you know what your uncle reminds me of?" Scott asked.

Victor felt Franklin's neck. The old man's pulse was slow but steady.

"He reminds me of this toy robot I got for Christmas. It's from Japan and it can walk over anything."

Victor nodded. "That's great, Scott."

"When its batteries run low, it walks just like your uncle. But when I put new batteries in," Scott continued, "it's like he's brand-new."

Victor paused. New batteries?

"Scott," said Victor. "You're a genius."

CHAPTER ELEVEN
Victor and Franklin Go Shopping

By six o'clock, Franklin was feeling much better. A steady charge of electricity from a couple of car batteries had done wonders for him, but this was only a temporary solution. Sooner or later, Victor's mom and Mrs. Vamos would try to start their cars and realize something was missing. Franklin needed better parts, and fast. Victor knew exactly where to find them. The old man insisted on tagging along.

As they walked along the sidewalk, Franklin lugged a battery under each arm. Jumper cables ran from the terminals up his sleeves to the bolts on his neck.

"Victor, your modern world is astounding. *Everything* is new. Even people look markedly different." Franklin noticed a black Belgian sheepdog tied to a lamppost in front of a barbershop. "But not dogs. Isn't that interesting? They are the same in any age."

Franklin dropped the batteries and crouched down to scratch the dog behind its ears. One of the cables snapped loose from his neck.

"Blast these infernal things," Franklin cursed. "Oh, I am sorry, Victor. Your solution is excellent. I don't mean to complain." He reached down his collar and fished around for the cable.

"Just a little longer, Ben," Victor said. "My cousin's hardware store is right over there. He's sure to have smaller batteries."

"Excellent," said Franklin. "But just the same, perhaps I should disconnect my cables while we are inside. I would hate to attract undue attention."

"I don't know. How do you feel?"

Franklin unclipped the other cable and stood up. "I feel fine, fully energized. Just as I did when I awoke from the Leyden casket."

"Interesting," said Victor. "Your body is functioning exactly like a rechargeable battery. I wonder how long you can hold a charge."

"It's difficult to say. When I awoke from my long sleep, I retained power for more than a week." Franklin smiled. "However, at that point I had been charging for more than two hundred years."

TOO MUCH POWER

Ben becomes a rampaging monster.
Eyes glow. Super strong!

RIGHT AMOUNT OF POWER

Ben thinks clearly.
Behaves like a normal human being.

NOT ENOUGH POWER

Ben becomes a zombie.
Eats electricity anywhere he can find it.

Victor pulled out a small pad of paper and scribbled some notes. "This is starting to make sense. The trick, I think, is for us to keep your electric state perfectly stable. We don't want too much or too little."

"But how can we do that?" asked Franklin.

"Don't worry. We just need a device to monitor your battery level and keep you steady. It's basic electronics. Come on. If Ernie has the parts, I think I can put something together."

Franklin gave the dog one last pat on the head, and then followed Victor into the store.

★ ★ ★

Ernie's was the best kind of hardware store. It was dark and dusty, and you never knew quite what you were going to find. If Victor's cousin didn't have exactly what you were looking for, he could probably rig something up.

A lumpy, balding man sat behind the counter, doing paperwork. He was wearing a bright Hawaiian shirt and plaid golf pants. Across his chest, he wore a bandolier, like a Mexican bandito. But instead of holding bullets, the loops on Ernie's belt were filled with pencils, tools, and Tootsie Rolls.

"Hey, Victor!" said Ernie. "What's the word, bird?"

"Hi, Ernie. I'm working on a project, and I'm going to need some parts."

"Cool," said Ernie. "Electric, steam, or nuclear powered?"

"Electric," said Victor. "Oh, and this is my neighbor, Mr. Benjamin. He's renting the apartment downstairs."

Ernie looked Franklin up and down. "Your friend has style, Victor."

On their way over, Victor and Franklin had stopped at the thrift store to find more modern clothes. Unfortunately, Franklin's size had limited their selection. The only things that fit had been a pair of lime green sweatpants and a turtleneck sweater with a picture of a bumblebee. To disguise his features, Victor had tied Franklin's hair back in a ponytail and given him a pair of sunglasses.

"Mr. B., your face looks familiar. Have we met?"

"I can't imagine where," said Franklin. Behind Ernie's head, a giant novelty hundred-dollar bill hung in a silver frame.

"Strange. I never forget a face. Anyway, you know where everything is, Victor. Feel free to look around."

Victor thanked Ernie and disappeared into the back of the store to rummage through the bins. At the counter, Ernie went back to work stapling piles of receipts together. Franklin stood by, watching with intense fascination.

"Something I can help you with, Mr. B.?"

"That device," said Franklin. "How does it work?"

"What device?"

"Your machine. The one you use to fasten the papers together."

Ernie looked up, a puzzled expression on his face. "You mean the stapler?"

Franklin nodded excitedly. "May I?"

Ernie shrugged and handed it over. "Knock yourself out."

Franklin examined the stapler from all angles. He held it up to the light and turned it around in his hands. He picked up a piece of paper and stapled it.

Benjamin Franklinstein Lives!

Ker-chunk!

Franklin laughed. "Fascinating. May I try again?"

"You're the customer."

Franklin began stapling the paper again, first slowly and then picking up speed, chuckling with glee.

Ker-chunk! Ker-chunk! Ker-chunk! Kerchunkerchunkerchunker—

The top sprang open and all the staples flew out onto the floor.

"Oh, I am sorry, sir!" said Franklin, scrambling to sweep up the mess. "Have I broken it?"

THE MODERN MECHANICAL STAPLER

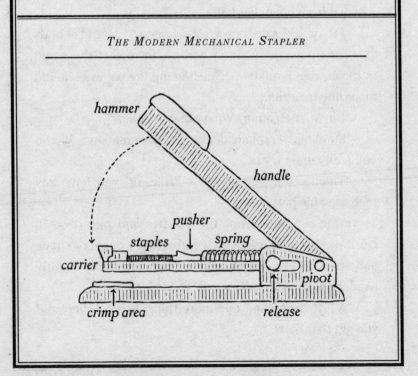

"No worries," said Ernie. "You really dig staplers, huh?"

"I do. Such an ingenious machine!"

Ernie nodded. "Listen, man, if you want, you can staple these receipts for me. No charge."

"You don't mind?"

"For a pal of Victor's?" said Ernie. "My pleasure."

Ernie refilled the stapler and Franklin set to work enthusiastically fastening the papers together. By the time Victor returned, he had finished the entire pile and was looking around for more paper.

"Find everything you need, kid?" asked Ernie, pulling a pencil from his bullet belt.

"I think so," said Victor. He dropped a crateful of odds and ends onto the counter and began to sort them out. In the corner, Franklin began stapling the pages of an old magazine together.

"Uh, Mr. Benjamin? What are you doing?"

"Stapling!" Franklin declared. "It's great fun. Victor, you really must try it."

"Thanks. Maybe later. Say, Ernie, do you have any rechargeable batteries?"

Ernie reached below the counter and pulled out a cardboard box overflowing with batteries of every shape and size. "You're in luck. Just got these in—only slightly used. How many do you want?"

"All of them. And one more thing, Ernie. Where did you get that belt?"

CHAPTER TWELVE
Vesuvius Destroyed

"I think that should do it," said Victor. He set down the soldering iron and inspected his work. "It's messy, but we can fix it later."

Ernie's bullet belt, now loaded with an arsenal of batteries, lay on Franklin's workbench. Each battery was linked to the next with red and black wire, and the whole series was patched into a small plastic box duct-taped to the buckle.

Franklin examined the belt with fascination. "How does it work?"

"It's pretty simple," said Victor, pulling out his cell phone. "See that box? I rigged it up last year to monitor the moisture content of the plants in my room. It sends me a text message when I need to water them."

"Text message?" said Franklin. "The box writes to you?"

"In a way." Victor held up his phone. "See these numbers? They will tell us where your charge is. Since you're not plugged in yet, they're all at zero."

"But once I am connected, you will be able to track my power?"

"In theory," said Victor. "But—"

"It is truly ingenious!" Franklin unclipped the cables from the car batteries and reached for the belt.

"Not so fast," said Victor. "I have a series of tests prepared, to be sure the readouts are properly calibrated and the sensors don't drift. It should be ready for a trial run in a couple of days."

"Or it might work perfectly right now," said Franklin, pulling the belt over his shoulder. "Victor, I simply can't function strapped to those large batteries. I need to resume repairing the electrophone right away. Where do I plug this in?"

"You don't," said Victor. "We need to wait until we're absolutely sure it's going to work. Right now, I would estimate our chance of success at less than—"

Franklin held up a finger. "Do not fear mistakes, Victor. If it doesn't work, we will simply try again. I have often found that failure is more instructive than success."

"I don't agree," said Victor.

Franklin smiled. "I know you don't. Now, I assume

these wires clip to my neck bolts? There! Now what does your device tell you?"

Victor checked his phone. "Nothing. I told you it wasn't ready."

Franklin unclipped the wires and reversed them. "And what does it say now?"

Victor's phone beeped, and a stream of numbers began to scroll across the display.

"It says we got lucky."

☆　☆　☆

Victor's mom had to work the evening shift again, so Victor brought his dinner down to the basement to eat while Franklin worked on the electrophone. The old man's cheery demeanor was starting to fade.

"Explain it to me again," said Victor. "How is it supposed to work?"

Franklin pointed to the glowing jars on the floor. "The Leyden jars collect the charge from the lightning rod. That charge powers the chromatic amplifier, which excites the harmonic fluid and sends pulses of Hyperion waves back up the signal chamber to the roof. I'm sure it all sounds ridiculously simple to you."

"Sort of," said Victor. "What part isn't working?"

"That's just it," said Franklin. "I have no idea. Everything seems to be functioning properly. But still, I'm not picking up a signal. It is most strange."

Victor nodded. "Ben, can I ask you something?"

"Of course, Victor."

"I was just thinking, what if the electrophone *is* working properly? What if the problem is at the other end?"

Franklin set aside his tools and sat down. "In other words, what if the Modern Order of Prometheus no longer exists? I have considered the possibility. The equipment on the roof has not been maintained. So why was I awakened?"

"Could it all just be an accident? The night you awoke, there was a weird storm. Lightning struck the house. Maybe that lightning bolt somehow tripped your circuit?"

"It is possible," said Franklin. "Perhaps even likely. But for now, I must assume that the Prometheans are out there somewhere, and they need me."

"I understand," said Victor. "How can I help?"

★ ★ ★

They worked into the evening, and Victor tried every trick he knew. Unfortunately, there were aspects of Franklin's unique technology that he still couldn't grasp. The harmonic fluid, for example. It powered the Leyden jars, the electrophone, and even Franklin himself. But what was it, exactly? Franklin did his best to explain. As far as Victor could understand, it was a sort of high-voltage oil. One day, when this was all over, he would have to sit Franklin down and have him explain it in detail.

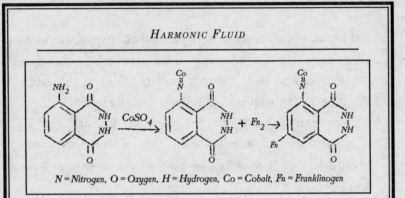

N = Nitrogen, O = Oxygen, H = Hydrogen, Co = Cobalt, Fn = Franklinogen

But the harmonic fluid wasn't the problem; he was pretty sure of that. His voltmeter showed that the electrophone was holding a steady charge, and he could even detect a change in the electrical fields when Franklin tried to broadcast. The whole thing appeared to be working properly.

Victor needed to clear his head and think about something else for a while.

"Hey, Ben, how would you like to see *my* invention?"

"An invention, eh?" Franklin set down his tools. "I suppose we could spare a minute or two."

Victor scrambled upstairs. Five minutes later he came back down and gently set his project on a workbench. It was concealed beneath a large red cloth. With a flourish, he pulled it back.

"What is it?"

"It's a volcano. Mount Vesuvius. It even erupts."

Victor explained how he had analyzed successful science fair projects from past years. "So you see, this baking soda volcano has a 97 percent chance of winning this year's fair. It's practically a sure thing."

Franklin studied Victor's project. "Tell me, Victor. What part of this invention did you actually invent?"

Victor hadn't expected the question. "Invent?"

"Yes, invent," Franklin said. "You called this your invention. But it sounds like you've just borrowed the work of others."

Victor had never thought of it that way.

"Well, *technically* I suppose I didn't invent any of it, but I don't want to risk entering something untested. You don't know these judges. They can be very fussy."

Franklin peeked into the volcano. "How does it work?"

"I put baking soda in this hole at the top," Victor explained. "When I add an acid, like lemon juice or vinegar, the baking soda foams up. It bubbles over like lava. It's very reliable."

"I see," Franklin said. "And what makes the fire?"

"Fire?"

"I assume there's fire. This is a volcano, isn't it?"

"None of the other projects had fire."

Franklin began rummaging through a cabinet, pulling bottles of colored powders from the shelves. One by one, he handed them to Victor.

"What are you doing?" Victor asked.

"Inventing!" He raced about the room. "I have an idea that will make your volcano come alive."

"I don't know. It's actually pretty much the way I want it right now."

"Trust me." The old man smiled. "I know something about invention. Bifocals? The artificial arm? The glass harmonica? Perhaps you've heard of them?"

"But I've been working on this for months." Victor swallowed.

"Never confuse motion with action, Victor. Now, here's what you do."

Franklin showed Victor how to mix the powders together. Reluctantly, Victor poured them into the top of the volcano.

"Now, for the magic. Where is my tinderbox?" Franklin scanned the room. "Never mind. I have a better idea. Step back and hold your nose."

The old man took three big gulps of air and—*BANG!*—burped at the volcano. Sparks shot from his mouth and ignited the powder.

First, it smoldered a little. Purple bubbles poured from the top. Suddenly, a jet of fire flashed straight up, narrowly missing Victor's face. Franklin yanked him back just in time.

Boiling lava foamed over the volcano and ran down its sides. The mouth of the volcano combusted, and a ring of fire spread toward the edges. Victor kicked the model to the floor and stamped out the flames, crushing what remained of his project. He watched as it melted into a black and purple lump.

He was flabbergasted.

Finally, he sputtered, "You . . . you ruined my project! And the science fair is in *four days*."

Franklin surveyed the mess. "Oh, Victor, I am sorry. I never meant to destroy your work."

They stood silently, staring at the charred lump on the floor.

Finally, Franklin spoke. "Still, in spite of everything, it was a fine volcano. If only for a moment."

Victor shook his head. He picked up the red cloth from the floor and shook off the ashes.

"Victor?"

"What."

"I never should have put your project at risk. Sometimes my enthusiasm gets the better of me."

"Whatever."

Franklin knelt and helped Victor collect the pieces. "You can still win. You can rebuild it. Let me help you."

"There's no time. Just forget it."

"Victor, I—"

"*Forget it.* Look, it was just a stupid volcano. I'm going up to bed. We'll work on the electrophone tomorrow, okay?"

"Of course, Victor. I am sorry."

"I know, Ben. See you in the morning."

CHAPTER THIRTEEN
Franklin Visits the Old Neighborhood

Victor woke to the sounds of voices in the kitchen.

"Of course, Mr. Benjamin. I'll be happy to draw you a map. Now, are you familiar with the bus routes? You'll probably need to make at least one transfer, maybe two."

"A transfer, yes, of course," said Franklin. "Remind me again how that works?"

Was Ben really planning to go into the city by himself? That would be disastrous.

Victor threw on some clothes and raced into the kitchen.

"Morning, Mom. Oh, hi, Mr. Benjamin. What's going on?" At the table, Franklin and Mrs. Godwin were poring over a city transit map. Franklin was dressed in his sweatpants and bumblebee sweater.

"Mr. Benjamin has an urgent appointment downtown today at the . . . what is it called again?"

"The American Philosophical Society, madam."

"Yes, of course. It's down near Independence Hall, but I'm afraid getting there will be more complicated than I thought."

"I know where that is," said Victor, sitting down across from them. "Maybe I can help."

Mrs. Godwin handed the map to Victor. "I don't know," she said. "I've been all over this. I'm not sure there's any easy route."

"No, I meant maybe I could take Mr. Benjamin there. I've always wanted to see the, uh, that place, and this could be my chance. Besides, helping him can count toward my volunteer hours for Junior Honor Society."

Mrs. Godwin shook her head. "The last time I checked, today was a school day."

"Mom, I haven't missed a day of school in four years. I'm ahead in all my classes, and my science fair project is . . . well, it's finished."

"I don't know." She turned to Franklin. "I doubt Mr. Benjamin wants you tagging along to his important meeting."

"On the contrary, Mrs. Godwin," said Franklin. "I would be honored to have Victor's assistance. As you can

Benjamin Franklinstein Lives!

see, I am a man of advanced years. To be quite honest, I fear making the trip alone."

"Well," Mrs. Godwin said, "I suppose—"

"Thanks, Mom," said Victor. "If there are any problems, we'll give you a call. Come on, Mr. Benjamin. If we hurry, we can catch the next bus."

★　　★　　★

Downstairs, Franklin paused at the door to his apartment.

"Victor, I want to thank you for this. After the way I ruined your volcano last night, it is more than I deserve. What will you do about the science fair?"

"I'm going to enter my ceramic insulator project," Victor said. "It won't win, but at least I'll get credit."

"Nonetheless," Franklin said, "I am in your debt."

"Forget about it. So what's so important at this philosophy place?"

"The American Philosophical Society," Franklin corrected. "If the Prometheans still exist, that is where they will be. I'll explain on the way. Right now, I want to collect my battery belt. It's been charging all night, as you recommended."

"Just a second," said Victor. "If you go out in public dressed like that, you're going to attract a lot of attention."

"What do you suggest?"

"How about your old clothes? We can hide the wires

and batteries better under your vest and coat. We'll dress you like Benjamin Franklin."

"But won't that attract even more notice?"

Victor smiled. "Not in Philadelphia."

★　★　★

Ten minutes later, they were on the sidewalk. Dressed in his colonial garb, Franklin looked magnificent. As they waited for the bus, Victor tried repeatedly to ask him about the Philosophical Society. All Franklin wanted to talk about was how a bus worked.

"I think I'm beginning to understand. You say there is a stove beneath the carriage that turns the wheels?"

"It's not really a stove," said Victor. The bus pulled up. He climbed the steps and handed their fare to the driver. "It's an engine. It burns fuel, and that moves the pistons. They turn the wheels."

"Fascinating," marveled Franklin. He stepped back off the bus and began to walk around the front. "Pistons, you say!"

"Ben, we don't have time." A large woman with several shopping bags squeezed between Victor and the driver.

"I can see the engine, Victor! Come look!" Franklin was on his knees now, peering beneath the wheel well.

More riders pushed their way through. The bus driver gave Victor a nasty look.

"Ben!" shouted Victor.

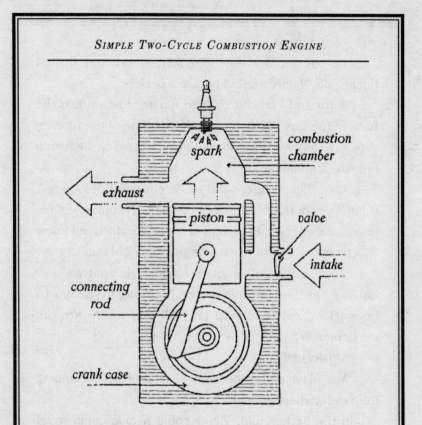

combustion chamber

spark

exhaust

piston

valve

intake

connecting rod

crank case

"Better tell your friend to move his butt," growled the driver. He honked the horn.

Franklin jumped back, amazed. "Victor! Did you hear that sound?"

"Give me one second," said Victor to the driver. He raced down the steps and grabbed Franklin by the jacket. "Ben, I promise I'll teach you all about internal combustion engines as soon as we get home. Right now, we have to get on this bus."

"Of course, my boy!" Franklin stood and dusted himself off. "I only wanted to take a peek."

Victor and Franklin claimed a pair of seats near the back of the bus. As Victor predicted, none of the passengers gave any notice to an old man dressed as Benjamin Franklin shuffling by.

"Look, Ben, I understand you're curious. But for now, I think it's important we stick to the plan." He pulled out his phone and checked Franklin's charge. "We still don't know exactly how long your power is going to hold out."

"True enough," said Franklin. He patted the battery belt beneath his jacket. "Although it seems to be working splendidly so far. Tell me, where are the musicians?"

"Musicians?"

"Yes, playing that peculiar song. It seems to be coming from everywhere at once."

In the background, Victor could hear a commercial for chewing gum. A woman was singing about fresh breath and flavor crystals. "Oh, that's just the radio. Those are speakers in the ceiling."

"Speakers? People speaking?"

"No, it's another machine. The speakers play the sound from the radio. Kind of like the electrophone."

"The electrophone? Then perhaps . . ." Franklin stood and climbed up onto his seat. Clutching a pole for support, he pressed his face to the speaker and began to whisper. "Prometheans, are you there? It is me, Dr. Franklin. I have awakened!"

"Ben," hissed Victor. "Sit *down!* People are staring."

The bus turned a corner and Franklin tumbled onto the floor. Several passengers offered to help him back into his seat, but Victor waved them off. Despite their precautions, the old man was still prone to giving off powerful shocks.

"You've got to be more careful, Ben. You could have gotten seriously hurt."

"The things which hurt instruct, my boy," said Franklin with a wink. "Next time I shall wait until the bus stops completely. Speaking of which, isn't this where we make our transfer?"

PHILOSOPHICAL HALL

Victor held his phone in front of him and studied the map. "According to the GPS, the American Philosophical Society should be right around the corner."

"That is truly a remarkable device, but you can put it away. We will have no need for it today." Franklin stormed ahead like a man in his twenties, pointing out landmarks with joyful satisfaction. "The Pennsylvania State House, of course it still stands. And here, just around the corner . . . do hurry, Victor . . . yes, Library Hall!"

Victor raced to keep up. He found Franklin standing in the center of Fifth Street, marveling at a two-story brick building.

"My friends from the Junto and I formed this library, Victor. The first in the nation! Forty shillings each, it cost us. A bargain, if I do say so myself."

"Junto?" asked Victor. "What was that?"

Franklin lowered his voice. "A secret organization, formed to discuss issues of morals, politics, and natural philosophy. The Junto grew into the American Philosophical Society, which met there, in Philosophical Hall." Franklin gestured to another brick building across the road. "It was a collective of the greatest scientific minds of our time."

"So you started the American Philosophical Society?"

Franklin laughed. "My boy, I built the building! Or, rather, I paid for it. I was also its first president.

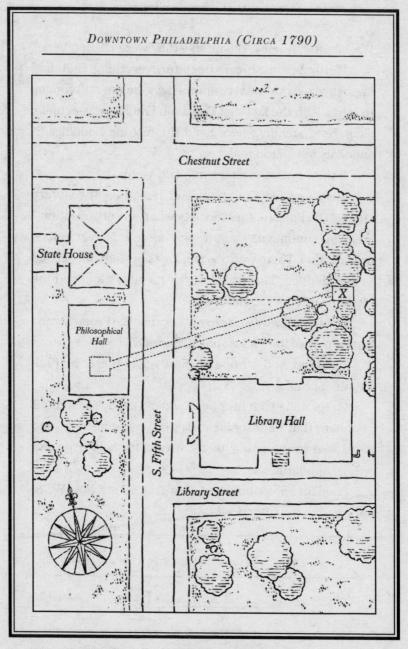

DOWNTOWN PHILADELPHIA (CIRCA 1790)

Chestnut Street

State House

Philosophical Hall

X

Library Hall

S. Fifth Street

Library Street

Washington, Adams, Hamilton—they were all members."

Victor felt a shiver. Despite everything that had happened over the past couple of days, he was still coming to terms with the fact that Benjamin Franklin was actually alive. Now, standing here amid the historic buildings, it suddenly felt all too real.

"I think I need to sit down," said Victor.

They crossed the street and rested on the library steps. "The Philosophical Society was a fine organization," Franklin continued, "but it was also a largely public organization. There were certain areas of study we needed to keep hidden. Thus, a select few members founded the Modern Order of Prometheus."

"And that's why we're here? Because the Prometheans were a part of the Philosophical Society?"

"Exactly. And I hope to find them there, at Philosophical Hall."

Victor pulled out his phone and did a quick search. "It says here that Philosophical Hall is a museum now. And it's closed to the public today, except for field trips and special appointments."

Franklin shook his head. "No matter, my boy. We're not going in the front door."

THE STANDARD CUSTODIAN'S SHOVEL

Benjamin Franklinstein Lives!

CHAPTER FOURTEEN
Trapped!

Franklin led Victor back up Fifth Street and into a small park behind Library Hall. Despite the early hour, groups of sightseers lined the brick paths. Franklin smiled at the children, bowed to the adults, and pressed on to the back corner of the park. There, under the shade of several large trees, was a small square building the size of a shed. The door was sealed with a padlock. Franklin gave it a tug.

"Victor, I trust you know how to open one of these?"

Victor took a deep breath. Locks of all kinds had fascinated him for years, and he recognized this as a particularly easy model to open. But lock picking had just been a hobby.

"I don't know, Ben. This is breaking and entering. We could go to jail."

"Nonsense! How can it be breaking and entering if I built the building?"

"You might have trouble convincing the police of that. You know, considering you died more than two hundred years ago."

"I see your point." He thought for a moment. "Then we must make sure we don't get caught. Leave it to me."

Franklin strode back to the center of the park, stood before a statue, and began to speak. "My friends, a penny saved is a penny earned! Haste makes waste! And he that speaks much, is much mistaken!"

A small crowd began to form, fascinated by the old man's spot-on impersonation of Benjamin Franklin.

It was now or never. Victor pulled out his pocketknife, took a quick glance around to make sure no one was watching, and set to work on the lock.

"Good sense is a thing all need, few have, and none think they want!" shouted Franklin.

The tumblers were rusty. Victor opened another tool on his knife and tried to loosen them. He was close, but his hands wouldn't stop shaking.

"Hunger is the best pickle!"

Snap! The lock popped open. As calmly as he could, Victor joined the crowd and signaled to Franklin.

". . . and that, my friends, concludes today's lesson.

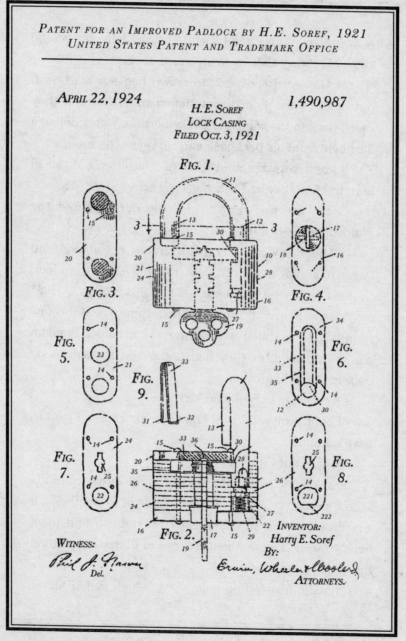

APRIL 22, 1924   1,490,987

H. E. SOREF
LOCK CASING
FILED OCT. 3, 1921

FIG. 1.

FIG. 3.

FIG. 4.

FIG. 5.

FIG. 6.

FIG. 9.

FIG. 7.

FIG. 2.

FIG. 8.

WITNESS:

Phil J. Hanson
Del.

INVENTOR:
Harry E. Soref
BY:
Erwin, Wheeler & Cooler
ATTORNEYS.

Now please join my good friend Thomas Jefferson on the steps of Library Hall for fresh-baked cookies!"

At the word *cookies,* the crowd began a mad dash out of the park. Franklin motioned to Victor, and they raced back to the shed and ducked inside. Victor pulled a flashlight from his backpack and surveyed the room.

It was full of rakes, shovels, bags of fertilizer, and a small lawn tractor. They had risked getting arrested for this?

"What are we going to do? Dig our way into the Philosophical Society?"

"Patience, Victor." Franklin grabbed a shovel and began to scrape at the dirt floor, tapping it every few feet. "It must be here somewhere. . . . Perhaps here? . . . Aha!"

Victor heard it too. The last thump was hollow sounding. He grabbed another shovel and helped Franklin dig. Within minutes they had uncovered a small metal door in the ground.

"A secret passage!" said Victor.

"I built it myself," said Franklin. "Or, rather, I paid to have it built."

"Where does it lead?"

Franklin smiled. "This, my boy, is the entrance to the secret sanctuary of the Modern Order of Prometheus. If any Prometheans still exist, we're certain to find them here. Now, let's hope this ladder is in better shape than the one in your basement."

Franklin insisted on going first, which suited Victor

just fine. But that also meant giving up the flashlight. Next time, he would have to remember to bring two.

The tunnel was wet and narrow, and it reminded Victor of pictures he had seen of old coal mines. Large wooden beams, reinforced with iron, crossed the ceiling every few feet. Rusty lanterns hung from hooks on the walls. He tried not to think about what might be living in the shadows.

Suddenly, the old man stopped and pushed Victor back with his hand. "Don't move! I nearly forgot!"

Franklin turned the flashlight to the ceiling. Victor could just make out three heavy chains running behind a beam, over pulleys, and down the wall.

"It's a trap," said Franklin. "Jefferson's invention. It was designed to keep intruders away. One wrong step, and two large gates will fall, sealing us in from both ends."

Victor froze. Suddenly, regular aboveground jail didn't sound so bad after all.

"But not to worry. There are three pulleys, you see, and numbers engraved into each link. If we simply line them up in the proper combination, the mechanism will release and disarm the trap. It's really very simple."

"What's the combination?" asked Victor hopefully.

Franklin paused. "Well now, that is a problem. At one point, it was the ages of the three founding members of the Order, but I'm fairly sure we changed it. I remember that another member proposed basing it on the orbit of

Venus, which was just ridiculous. No, it was something much simpler to remember . . ."

Franklin tipped his head and stared at the chains. Minutes passed, and Victor could feel his legs falling asleep. He didn't dare step forward, fearing he might set off the trap.

"If it were me," offered Victor, "I might have used a cipher. That's what I do with most of my combinations."

"Of course!" said Franklin. "That makes much more sense. But a cipher of what?"

Victor shrugged. "Something with three letters, like, I don't know . . . *M—O—P*, for Modern Order of Prometheus?"

Franklin immediately began to tug on the chain. "Yes! *M* is the—let me see—thirteenth letter of the alphabet, so we'll pull this one to thirteen. Then *O* is . . ."

"Ben!" shouted Victor. "I didn't mean that you should actually do it. It was only a silly guess!"

"It was an excellent guess," said Franklin. "And how will we know unless we try? Besides, I'm fairly certain that setting the wrong combination won't *immediately* release the gates. It never did before. Now, if *O* is the fifteenth letter, *P* is the seventeenth."

"Sixteenth!" Victor could feel the panic setting in.

"Yes, the sixteenth." Franklin chuckled. "Where is my mind today? So there we have it: thirteen-fifteen-sixteen. Shall I give it a go?"

Without waiting for an answer, Franklin pulled the last chain. He paused a moment, and when nothing happened, he set off down the tunnel. "See? I told you it would work."

A minute later, the flashlight's beam was only a dim glow far ahead. "It's okay, my boy!" Franklin shouted. "We've done it! Come along!"

Gingerly, Victor took a single step forward. Was it possible? Had he actually cracked the code? It seemed too simple.

And then he heard the squeak, as if a wheel somewhere was turning and needed oil.

"Ben? Did you hear that?"

"I did. It seems we may have entered the wrong combination after all. Perhaps you should walk a bit more briskly, Victor."

Victor bolted down the tunnel toward Franklin's voice, his feet slipping in the soft mud. He could hear the chains spinning on their pulleys. Ahead, a metal gate descended from the ceiling.

"Faster, my boy! You can do it!"

As the gate fell, he dived at the flashlight's beam and skidded on his belly along the wet, muddy floor, like a runner sliding headfirst into third base. His face slammed hard into Franklin's leg. Behind his feet, the metal bars locked into place with a clang.

Franklin laughed. "It still works! My word, have you

ever seen such a contraption? Say what you will about Jefferson, he was a fine inventor."

Victor struggled to his feet. His sweatshirt and pants were coated in foul-smelling mud. "Ben, we could have been trapped in there! We could have died!"

"I doubt it," said Franklin. "We're smart fellows, you and I. We would have figured something out."

"But—"

"No buts, Victor. We have had our fun, and now there is work to do. We have arrived!"

Franklin shined the flashlight on the far end of the tunnel. Victor could see another ladder leading back to the surface. "Where does it go?"

"Prepare yourself!" said Franklin, charging ahead. "You are about to meet members of the most secret society on Earth. It is an honor few have received."

As Victor struggled to wipe chunks of mud from his clothes, Franklin bounded up the ladder like an acrobat. Victor scrambled behind. He arrived just in time to see Franklin forcing open a hatch above his head.

"I think it's stuck," said Franklin. He pushed again with all his strength. Victor could hear wood splintering. Suddenly, the hatch gave way and light streamed in from above.

"What is it?" said Victor. "What do you see?"

"Victor," said Franklin, "we may have a problem."

CHAPTER FIFTEEN

Too Many Franklins

In the downstairs cafeteria of the American Philosophical Society Museum, a small group of schoolchildren gathered to eat their mid-morning snacks. It had already been a busy day. They had seen a film about famous explorers and a skeleton from a real duck. Now, the head of Benjamin Franklin was peering back at them from a hole in the floor.

"Are you a troll?" asked one of the children.

"Look, it's a troll!" shouted a girl, her mouth full of peanut butter and jelly. Several children began to scream.

"Quick," whispered Victor. "Close the hatch!"

"The gates are down, Victor. We can't go back." Franklin pushed the hatch the rest of the way open and squeezed his way up through the hole, into the cafeteria. All around, children were clapping their hands and squealing with delight.

"Hello, children," said Franklin, nodding. "My name is Benjamin Franklin."

"Benjamin Franklin is dead!" shouted a little boy with glee. "You're dead!"

In the back of the room, a confused museum guide shuffled through her papers. Was this part of the program?

"It is indeed a pleasure to meet you all," Franklin said, dusting himself off. "I hope you are enjoying your day."

"Do you live down there?" asked a girl. "Is that your son? Why is he all dirty?"

Victor cautiously pulled himself up from the tunnel and then slid the tile back into place. In the back of the room, he could see the museum guide making a phone call.

"I wish I could stay and answer all your questions," said Franklin, "but my good friend John Adams is waiting for me at the library. Victor, shall we go?"

Victor nodded, and followed Franklin as he headed for the door. Maybe, just maybe, if they moved quickly . . .

"Excuse me, sir?" A security guard had appeared suddenly from around the corner and was now blocking the door. "Are you allowed to be here? I'll need to see some identification."

"Allowed to be here?" said Franklin. "Young man, I *built* this building. Or rather, I paid to have it—"

"You'll have to excuse my friend," interrupted Victor. "Once he's in costume, he really becomes the character. It's part of his training."

The guard nodded. "How exactly did you get into the building, sir?"

"He came up through the floor," offered one of the schoolchildren. "He lives down there with his son."

"I see." The guard turned to Victor. "And what happened to you, exactly?"

"I slipped," said Victor. "Outside."

"Look, gentlemen, I'm not sure exactly what's going on here, but I intend to find out." The guard pulled out his walkie-talkie. "Have a seat while I check with my supervisor."

"Of course," said Franklin. He winked at Victor. "We'll wait over there, in the . . . in the . . . *now, Victor! Run!*"

In a flash, Franklin was past the guard and racing up the steps. For a moment, Victor and the guard both froze in surprise. Victor recovered first and took off up the stairs. The schoolchildren cheered.

"Left, Victor—no, *right!* They've changed the building since I was here last." Franklin raced through exhibits, past startled workers, Victor hot on his heels.

"There! An emergency exit!" Victor grabbed Franklin's jacket and yanked him toward the door.

"Halt!" shouted the guard from somewhere behind. "Or I'll call the police!"

This time Victor didn't hesitate. He threw his weight into the handle. Alarm bells rang, lights flashed, and the door flew open. Suddenly, they were back outside, in a small alley beside Independence Hall.

"That way," said Victor. "It's our only chance!"

As they sprinted down the path, Victor scanned the park. He saw a man dressed as Benjamin Franklin selling cheesesteak sandwiches. Behind him, a group of tourists was listening to a lecture on the Liberty Bell. Victor reached into his pocket and pulled out a five-dollar bill.

"Buy yourself a sandwich and see if you can start a conversation with that guy. I'm going to join those kids."

Victor yanked off his muddy sweatshirt and tossed it behind a tree. As casually as he could, he strolled across the lawn and joined the tourists. In the distance, he could see the museum guard running their way.

Along the path, a strange scene was forming. Benjamin Franklin was buying a sandwich from Benjamin Franklin, while another Benjamin Franklin sold balloons on the sidewalk beside them. A short distance away, a fourth Benjamin Franklin was riding a unicycle and handing out flyers.

The museum guard paused, trying to make sense of what he was seeing. He took off his cap and wiped his brow. Finally, he shook his head and turned back toward the museum.

"Quick, Ben!" shouted Victor. "I think I see our bus."

"In good time, my boy," said Franklin, wiping grease off his chin with his sleeve. "But first, how about another sandwich?"

THE PHILADELPHIA CHEESESTEAK SANDWICH

Melted cheese or processed cheese food

Chopped steak (or vegetarian equivalent)

Hoagie roll

Optional ingredients: sauteed or fried onions, green peppers, and/or mushrooms

CHAPTER SIXTEEN
Lemonade

By the time they got back to the old man's apartment, Victor was exhausted and Franklin was stuffed from his cheesesteaks. Stuffed and disappointed.

"I fear the worst, Victor." Franklin sighed. "Although our visit to Philosophical Hall may have been invigorating, I can't help but feel that we have reached a dead end."

"A dead end?" Victor was stunned. "You're not giving up, are you?"

"The secret sanctuary was abandoned, Victor! Why, it wasn't even the secret sanctuary anymore. It was some sort of dining hall. For children, no less!"

"Things can change over a couple of hundred years," Victor said. "Maybe the Prometheans moved. We should keep transmitting on the electrophone. Eventually, someone's bound to answer."

"My boy, I appreciate your optimism, but we must face facts. Why would the Prometheans awaken me and not tell me where they've gone? It makes no sense." Franklin stood and walked to the window. "I should have known the moment I awoke without a Custodian at my side. Victor, you are looking at the last Promethean, accidentally revived by a freak bolt of lightning. I am simply an old man, lost in time."

Victor put a hand on Franklin's shoulder. "I'm still not ready to give up, Ben. As long as there's even a slight possibility that the Order survives, I want to help you find them."

Franklin smiled. Victor noticed his eyes widen ever so slightly. "Victor, you've already done more than your share. You've been so generous with your time and effort, but I have done very little for you. Except destroy your volcano, of course."

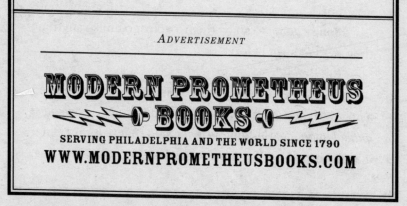
CHAPTER SIXTEEN: *Lemonade*

Victor winced at the thought.

"When is your science fair?" said Franklin. "Another week or so?"

"Three days. What does it matter?"

"You deserve to win. Let me assist you in building a new volcano."

"Absolutely not. We have more important work to do."

Franklin sighed. "Victor, if it will make you happy, let us strike a deal: I will agree to continue on this foolish quest to find the Order, but you must give me the opportunity to make amends for my mistake."

"Ben, even if I did agree, my last volcano took months to perfect. There's no way I could rebuild it in three days."

"I'm not proposing you rebuild it, Victor. I'm proposing you *reinvent* it. Make a *new* one, a better one!"

"Impossible. That one had a 97 percent chance of winning."

"Perhaps." Franklin leaned in close. "But that statistic was based on projects the judges had already seen."

"So?"

"You're going to show them a volcano unlike anything they've ever seen before!"

"But Ben—"

"Wait! I feel an aphorism coming on." Franklin raised a finger in the air. "*When life gives one lemons . . . one must make lemonade! Has anyone ever said that before?* I claim it as my own! Now, we must move fast. To work!"

1 3/4 cups fresh-squeezed lemon juice
(about 10 lemons)
2/3 cup honey
about 5 1/2 cups cold water

1. To squeeze the lemons, first roll them firmly between your hand and the counter to help release the juice. Cut the lemons in half and squeeze using a citrus juicer.

2. Combine the lemon juice and honey in a half-gallon pitcher.

3. Add enough cold water to make half a gallon. Important: Be sure to stir for at least 3 minutes to dissolve the honey.

4. Pour over ice in tall glasses. Enjoy!

CHAPTER SEVENTEEN
The Science Fair

It was, without a doubt, the ugliest project Victor had ever built. It stood eleven feet tall and seven feet in diameter. Its walls were a lumpy mass of two-by-fours, tempera paint, and papier-mâché. In the end, they had hacksawed it into pieces to get it out of the house, into Mrs. Godwin's station wagon, and into the Philo T. Farnsworth Middle School gymnasium. Now, hastily duct-taped back together, it was a mess, like a giant version of something Scott Weaver would make.

But its true mystery lay within. At first, Victor had tried to keep it simple, as close to his original model as possible. But at every opportunity, Franklin had challenged him to push it further. It was big, yes, but couldn't it be bigger?

And louder? And whoever heard of a volcano without smoke?

Building the volcano had been an exhausting blur. Under Franklin's coaching, Victor had called upon every scientific trick he knew. He added an elaborate system of pipes and hydraulics. He improved the lava chemistry with strange powders and liquids from Franklin's laboratory. And he powered the entire device with a complex electrical system they still hadn't fully tested.

There hadn't even been time to add any fleeing victims in togas carrying dogs. That was sure to cost them points with the judges. But there was no looking back. The science fair was about to start.

"Look at the time," Mrs. Godwin said. "I was supposed to be at the refreshment stand ten minutes ago. Don't get into too much trouble."

"We shall be most cautious, Mrs. Godwin," Franklin promised.

Mrs. Godwin hugged her son. "Good luck, Victor. You'll do great."

Victor wasn't so sure. "Thanks, Mom."

She disappeared into the crowd. The gym was packed with students and their families. Each student was setting up a project. Above them, a giant banner hung across the back wall: FARNSWORTH MIDDLE SCHOOL 34TH ANNUAL MANDATORY SCIENCE FAIR.

Franklin's eyes grew wide. "To see so many people—

children, yet!—gathered to celebrate science. It fills my heart with delight! How is my charge?"

Victor checked the display on his cell phone. "You're currently at 91 percent. You should function perfectly for several hours."

With Victor pushing and Franklin pulling, they rolled the volcano slowly across the gym.

Franklin was constantly distracted by the other projects. One in particular fascinated him.

Angela Willbrant had dressed her pet poodle, Caesar, in aluminum foil and strapped two long antennas to its head. Each antenna was capped with a Styrofoam ball. Taped to the dog's nose was a small blinking light, which

---

SELECTED PROJECTS FROM THE 34TH ANNUAL MANDATORY SCIENCE FAIR

Caesar kept trying to eat. The project was called "Are Dogs from Mars?"

Franklin turned to Victor, a puzzled look on his face. "They aren't, are they?"

Victor shook his head.

Finally, they found their assigned area. It was smaller than they had anticipated. Victor wedged the volcano forward into their space, nearly toppling the projects on the neighboring tables.

"Ben, you check the electrical system while I look for a place to hook this up." He grabbed a cable from under the volcano and went in search of an outlet.

When he returned, Franklin was gone.

Victor scanned the crowd until he spotted him. The old man was across the aisle, leaning over a large plastic garbage can.

"Hey, Victor!" Scott Weaver said, waving him over. "I was just talking to your uncle." He leaned in close and added, "He sure looks better than the last time I saw him."

"Astounding, simply astounding!" Franklin marveled. "Victor, you must see this!"

Inside the garbage can, hundreds of silver potatoes floated in a strange pink liquid. Every potato was pierced with nails, magnets, and assorted metallic objects from Scott's garage. Wires connected each metal contact in a massive web. The potatoes appeared to be glowing.

"I call it Potato Battery 2000. Do you like it?"

Victor reached in to examine one of the potatoes.

"Ouch!" He yanked his hand back.

"Sorry," said Scott. "I should have warned you. I put ketchup and some energy drinks in there to turn the potatoes red, but now it just gives you shocks. Cool, huh?"

"The marvel of it." Franklin seemed hypnotized by the glowing pink goo. "To think that mankind has finally harnessed the power of the potato! This is truly a glorious age. And you, young Scott, are an inventor of the first order."

Victor sighed. "Ben, it's time for us to go. It's almost our turn."

"I'll join you in just a moment, Victor." Franklin reached in and touched a potato. A single blue spark crackled at his fingertip.

★ ★ ★

Victor stood alone in front of the volcano. Where was Ben? This whole thing had been his idea. The least he could do was be here to help start it up. Not that it would work anyway. With all the compromises and changes—and no time to test it—Victor gave this volcano a less than 7 percent chance of winning.

The judges, four women and two men, moved to Victor's booth. Each one held a clipboard and a number two pencil. They circled the volcano, studying it silently. Finally, one of them spoke.

"It certainly is . . . big."

"Thank you," said Victor. He knew they hated it.

"Tell me, Victor, do you have a graph?"

The graph! How could he have forgotten the graph? He shook his head.

The judges murmured to each other and made notes on their clipboards.

"Victor," another judge said, "may I make a suggestion? Next time, start a little earlier. Your volcano is big, but it's awfully rough around the edges. You might have painted over the duct tape. And if this is Vesuvius, we should see details, like people in togas, running for their lives. Maybe even a little dog or two."

"And a graph," said the first judge. "It really needs a graph."

For a moment, everyone stood without saying anything. Finally, one judge asked, "Does it do anything?"

Victor swallowed. At this point, he had nothing to lose. "It does. Should I turn it on?"

"If you'd like."

Victor walked to the back of the volcano. He lifted part of the papier-mâché and reached inside for the button. He closed his eyes and pressed.

It worked better than he had ever imagined it would.

At first.

CHAPTER EIGHTEEN
Vesuvius Reborn

The button was connected to an old coffeemaker deep inside the volcano. When Victor switched it on, the harmonic fluid in the magma began to heat up. He couldn't see it working, but he could smell it. It was a strange scent, like someone lighting a match in a doughnut shop. So far, so good.

After about a minute, the sides of the volcano began to bulge. The smell was pungent now. People from nearby booths stopped what they were doing and began to sniff the air. The judges made notes on their clipboards.

Suddenly, one of the duct-taped seams on the side of the volcano split open, and reddish steam shot out. Victor held his breath. Red was good. It meant the valves had opened and the catalyst had entered the heating chamber. The base of the volcano began to shake. Everything was going pretty much as he and Franklin had planned.

Inside, the magma kept cooking. When it passed a hundred degrees, a temperature sensor closed a relay. This switched on the amplifier and speakers, and a deep, thunderous rumble filled the gym. The noise had been Franklin's idea, inspired by the sounds coming from his stomach. The judges nodded in approval.

Everyone was watching now. Everyone, Victor noted, except Franklin, who was still captivated by Scott Weaver's project. Victor shouted to him over the roar.

The smell was almost unbearable, and Victor stepped back. It was all about the tubes now. If the joints held and nothing melted, the eruption should begin in about—

BOOOOOOOOOOOOOOOOOOOOOOOOOOOOOM!

The top of the volcano exploded upward like fire from the mouth of a dragon. A reddish cloud of steam and smoke began to fill the ceiling of the gym as pieces of cardboard ash rained down upon the spectators. Victor laughed. It was all perfectly safe, but the effect was so convincing that even he couldn't help but cover his head.

But where was Ben? He was about to miss the best part.

Victor called to him again, but there was no response. The old man was lost in thought, examining a pink potato with intense curiosity.

Suddenly, a cheer rose up across the gym. The lava

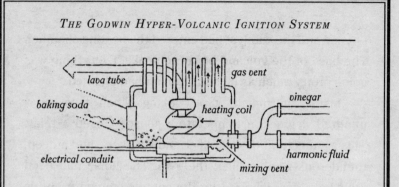

had begun to flow. A fountain of bright red foam gushed from the top of the mountain and spilled down the sides. As it cooled, each stream hardened and turned black. More lava flowed over the top, and the entire volcano began to slowly grow. The effect was hypnotic.

The judges had stopped writing and were staring, transfixed, at the awesome sight. There were smiles on their faces. Maybe, just maybe, Victor thought, he could win this thing after all.

The volcano grew bigger by the second. It was now at least a foot thicker than it had been, and the lava showed no sign of slowing down. The judges stepped back as it began to spill onto the floor at their feet.

Victor rubbed the back of his neck. Now would be a good time for the lava to stop. Why wasn't it stopping? Should he pull the plug? Before he could decide, he heard a commotion behind him.

"He's on fire!"

The cry had come from somewhere near Scott's

table. Victor's phone buzzed. Franklin's batteries were overcharging!

Victor climbed a chair for a better view. Franklin was not on fire, but he was sparking. His skin glowed. Smoke flowed from his ears and his eyes burned red. The old man stumbled blindly from side to side, his arms stretching forward, locked at the elbows, as he crashed into people and projects. Bits of potato hung from the side of his mouth.

Suddenly, he lunged forward, directly into Scott Weaver's project. The garbage can toppled. Potatoes and pink liquid spilled across the floor. Franklin fell to his knees and began to shove potatoes into his mouth as quickly as he could.

"Ben!" shouted Victor. "Stop! You're overloading!"

"MMMMMMORE!" Franklin cried. *"HUNGRY!"*

Meanwhile, the volcano continued to erupt.

The judges were trapped. The lava was flowing even faster now, and their only hope was to flee to higher ground. One by one, they climbed onto a small folding table, clutching one another for support. Below them, the strange foam kept rising.

Victor raced over to Franklin and began to kick the potatoes aside. Franklin was beyond reason. He splashed about in the puddle at his feet, searching frantically for more potato batteries to eat. Behind him, the lava began to flow toward the strange pink goo.

And then things went very, very wrong.

Benjamin Franklin burped.

Blue sparks shot from his mouth and the Potato Battery 2000 mixture erupted. A trail of fire raced across the floor. Flames shot up Franklin's sleeves and ignited his jacket. He lurched to his feet, confused. Now he really was on fire.

"FIRE BAADDD!"

Panicked, Franklin charged across the gym, trying to escape the flames. Anything that stood in his path was instantly pulverized. Lunch tables, the judges' podium, and a cotton candy machine were reduced to a mangled mess.

Across the gym, people screamed and raced for the exits.

Victor ripped the Mandatory Science Fair banner from the wall. He threw it over Franklin's glowing body and tried to smother the flames.

The jacket stopped burning. Draped in the white banner, Franklin paused, stunned but unhurt.

"The volcano!" someone screamed. "It's alive!"

Victor spun around. The goo from Scott Weaver's project had mixed with the lava. A bubbling chemical reaction was spreading across the volcano, turning it green. As the lava flowed from the top, foamy tree-shaped tendrils began to form. It looked to Victor like the volcano was growing hundreds of monstrous fingers, each one reaching and probing in a different direction.

Green clouds filled the air as the crowd raced for the exits. One by one, the judges jumped from their table into the sticky mess, abandoning their clipboards and pencils. The volcano, now three times its original size, was growing fast.

Victor knew what he had to do. He pulled his T-shirt up over his mouth and nose and headed straight into the storm. It was like trying to run through a sea of gum. The bubbling lava tugged at his sneakers. Each step was an eternity.

A voice on the loudspeaker urged everyone to evacuate in an orderly fashion. The smoke was making it hard to see. Emergency lights flashed from every wall, but they didn't seem to help. Where was that electrical outlet?

At last he found it, behind a toppled chair. Victor grabbed the cord and yanked it from the wall. The sounds from the amplifier immediately stopped. The volcano was off.

But the lava kept flowing, and the tendrils continued to grow.

Victor cursed. Somehow, he had measured the mixture wrong. There was no telling how long it would continue to react. He scanned the room for Franklin, but the thick smoke made it impossible to see.

He took one last look at the catastrophe he had created, and then fled for the nearest door.

CHAPTER NINETEEN

Franklinstein Triumphant

In the parking lot, the rescue personnel had already arrived. Firefighters leaped from their trucks and began to set up their equipment as police officers raced to cordon off the area.

"Step aside, kid!" the lead firefighter barked at Victor as he ran past, a length of hose slung over his shoulder.

Victor stumbled back, overwhelmed by all that was happening around him.

In the middle of the madness, several teachers tried to take a head count. It appeared that everyone was safe, but Angela Willbrant was in tears.

"Caesar!" she sobbed. "He's still inside!"

Somehow, Angela's dog had been lost in the panic.

Victor watched as another teacher urgently explained the problem to a firefighter. It didn't look good. The foam was rising through the gym windows. Green smoke poured out the front doors, and a strange smell permeated the parking lot. No one seemed sure of how to proceed.

This was all Victor's fault. He sat down on the curb and put his head in his hands. How could things have gone so wrong so quickly? His volcano of destruction. Ben's rampage. And now Angela's dog, trapped in the lava. If anything happened to Caesar, he would never forgive himself.

Victor stood up and surveyed the crowd. His mother was standing on the other side of the parking lot behind a police barrier. She craned her neck, straining to see her son. He waved to let her know he was okay.

But where was Ben? Had he survived? If anything had happened to him, Victor didn't know what he would—

CRASH!

Suddenly, there he was—a hulking, glowing figure, smashing through a window, riding a wave of lava. The white banner was still wrapped around Franklin's body like a toga. In his arms, he cradled a small foil-covered dog.

For a moment, the crowd stood stunned, gawking at the strange sight.

Then, all at once, everyone—the judges included—erupted in thunderous applause.

CHAPTER TWENTY

Last of the Prometheans

From the curb, Victor and Scott watched the firefighters extinguishing the last of the volcano.

"That was, without a doubt, the coolest thing I have ever seen," said Scott. "I mean ever. You're definitely going to win this year."

"I doubt it," said Victor. The entire gym floor and half the parking lot were covered in lava. Students struggled to carry what was left of their projects out to their cars. Victor calculated that his odds of winning had now dropped below zero percent.

"It was pretty neat, though," said Victor. "I'll give you that."

"Think you'll get in trouble?"

"Definitely." At the gym doors, Mrs. Godwin was talking to the principal, the fire chief, and several teachers.

"I wish just one of my projects would blow up like that," Scott said. "On purpose, I mean."

"Your potatoes were great, Scott. I'm sorry they got ruined."

Scott shrugged. "No big deal. Wait until you see what I'm going to make next."

"What?"

"I haven't figured it out yet. I thought I might try sweet potatoes and toothpaste this time. And holograms. And even more magnets. Want to help?"

Victor smiled. "Sounds like fun. Count me in."

"May I join you boys?"

Victor looked up. "Ben! How are you feeling?"

"You mean Frank," corrected Scott. "His name is Frank Benjamin. It's like Benjamin Franklin, but backward. That's how I remember it."

"Of course," said Victor. "How are you feeling, Frank?"

"Better now." He unbuttoned his vest. Beneath, the batteries on his belt had melted into black blobs. "Although I'm afraid your magnificent invention is ruined."

"Cool!" said Scott.

Victor examined the belt. "The batteries must have absorbed the charge from the potatoes."

"That would explain why I recovered so quickly."

Franklin scanned the parking lot. "Are the police gone?"

"I think so. They were here a while ago, making sure we were all okay. Did they talk to you?"

"I wasn't ready to answer their questions, so I hid behind a bush." He turned to Scott. "Young man, I wonder if you wouldn't mind giving me the recipe for those potatoes. I found them most invigorating."

A confused look crossed Scott's face. "Recipe?"

"Yes, that marvelous pink liquid. How did you make it?"

"I just sort of threw things in. You know, until something happened."

"Ah, experimenting." Franklin sat down on the curb next to Victor. As he did, he let out a soft electric burp. "I approve!"

"When you were behind the bush, did you happen to hear what my mom and the principal were talking about?" Victor asked. "Is she mad?"

"She is," Franklin said. "But also, I think, a little proud."

"Proud?"

"It seems everyone is most curious about how the lava works. They say they have never seen anything quite like it."

Victor laughed. "It was pretty impressive, wasn't it?"

"It was a remarkable achievement."

"But it failed."

"In a most spectacular fashion!" Franklin laughed. His face turned serious. "I am sorry, Victor."

"Don't be. It was totally worth it."

Victor was surprised by his own answer.

The firefighters were packing up to leave. Several custodians were hosing down the parking lot.

"We need to get you back home," said Victor. "We have no idea what your charge is. Besides, someone may be calling on the electrophone."

"I made an electrophone once," said Scott, "but it melted."

"Victor, I feel fine. And as for the electrophone, I will honor our bargain, but understand that I have made peace with my fate. I am happy to be living in such a fine century. Science and democracy are flourishing, and I am excited to learn more in the time I have left." Franklin smiled at Victor and Scott. "And I have already made friends."

"But you must be disappointed," said Victor. "I mean, you were supposed to awaken to solve a great problem."

"Who is to say I haven't? Let me ask you something, Victor. Are you disappointed that you had to build a new volcano?"

"No."

"And what will you do next year?"

"I was thinking about that. First thing, we need to fix the chemical makeup of the lava. It's all wrong. If we can tweak the flash point, the explosion could be even bigger.

And if we can figure out exactly what it was in Scott's potato battery that caused those awesome tendrils, we might have something truly great."

Scott grinned.

"That doesn't sound like a guaranteed recipe for success," said Franklin. "In fact, it sounds like a bit of a risk."

Victor shrugged. "Maybe science is supposed to be risky. Otherwise, you wouldn't learn anything new, right?"

Franklin smiled. "You sound like a man I once knew, many lifetimes ago. He risked his life to send me here today. To hear you speak those words warms my heart."

Franklin pulled one of Scott's potatoes from his coat pocket.

"Ben!" Victor said. "You're not going to eat another one of those things, are you?"

"Science is risk," Franklin said, taking a small nibble. "Besides, these are *delicious*!"

Benjamin Franklinstein Lives!

EPILOGUE

Meanwhile, deep in the basement of the Godwin house:

Bzzz . . . crackle . . . "Hello?" . . . *crackle . . .* "Hello? Dr. Franklin?" . . . *bzzzt . . .* "Dr. Franklin, are you there?"